What You Makes DIE

www.apexbookcompany.com

What Makes You DIE

Tom Piccirilli

An Apex Publications Book

Lexington, Kentucky

WHAT MAKES YOU DIE
ISBN: 978-1-937009-12-0
Copyright © 2013 by Tom Piccirilli
Cover Design © 2013 by Danni Kelly
Komodo Dragon Illustration © 2013 by Justin Stewart
Typography by Maggie Slater

Published by Apex Publications, LLC
PO Box 24323
Lexington, KY 40524

www.apexbookcompany.com

o

For everyone with an irrepressible rage or
shame, a sickly hue to your face or another's, a
half-forgotten heartache, a mistake that can
never be mended, a wound that can't be found,
a parent you can no longer cry to, an unending
lament, a dark angel with outstretched hand,
What Makes You Die is for you–

o

No screaming this time. Nobody drying out with the DTs, no meth-mouths groaning through black teeth. I kept my eyes shut and willed myself through the walls.

I tried to listen in on the group therapy sessions, the arts and crafts lessons where the patients proudly displayed their ceramic ashtrays. I heard the distant rhythmic taps of a ping pong game. The laugh track to a sitcom. There was a day room where patients could congregate. Not all psych hospitals had them. I could smell a hint of marijuana in the air from when the orderlies toked in the distant corners of hallways. The rest of the freaks, depressives, hysterics, deficients, nymphos, nyctophobes, catatonics, chronic masturbators, and paranoids went about their business and kept up with their muttering, hand-wringing, floor-licking, wall-glaring, and carrot-waxing.

I eased my eyes open. I was in the bin again, strapped to the bed railings, surrounded by family, about half of whom were actually there. The rest were dead, drifting in and out, sometimes smiling knowingly, sometimes just giving me hard looks of disappointment. My old man had been gone since I was seven but I remembered him better than anyone or anything, even my own face. My dead older brother Bobby gave me his profile, staring off like he had important things to think about.

The straps hadn't been needed for a couple of years now, since the last time I'd tried to off myself. I had a four-inch jagged scar on the left side of my belly where I'd tried to commit hara-kiri with a steak knife one Christmas Eve. I'd managed to plunge the blade in and drag it nearly four inches left to right. Four inches wasn't bad for a white, pudgy coward who knew nothing about the samurai code of Bushido except what he had seen in martial arts flicks. The ER docs had been impressed with my single-mindedness. So was I, especially after they told me I'd lost four feet of small intestine. I hadn't done much in the world, but at least I'd done that.

There was another face among the dead. Not new, but someone I hadn't seen or thought about since the ninth grade. It was Tony Todesco. He'd been my best friend for a summer or two around then. He'd been the most mature of any of our neighborhood gang and had gotten a job as a paperboy while the rest of us begged allowances from our parents. Tony had been flush with comic books and baseball cards and always had cash for the game room at the South Shore Mall.

He'd been clipped on his bike one morning on Old Miller Road and smeared along the curb for about fifty feet. We'd all gone down there to see where it had happened. Somebody had tried to wash the blood away but the summer sun had already baked the stains deep into the cement. The red was there for months. Whenever we drove by in my mother's Pinto she would give a brief moan of sympathy and touch the little plastic statue of Mary stuck on the dashboard.

Now Tony was standing beside my bed, his wild blond hair a mess like always, hanging in his blue eyes, a deep July tan giving him a nice healthy golden glow. What he might represent I had no idea. The regrets of my lost childhood, the cynicism of blood, the unforgivable sin of suicide when so many stolen lives abounded. But here he was again, somebody else out of my past come visiting.

WHAT MAKES YOU DIE

My ex-wife used to get so spooked by my drunken complaints about being haunted that she once called in some supernatural investigators from a TV show she liked. She wrote them an impassioned letter about our house being beset by evil forces, and they showed up with a ten-man film crew and a thirty-five-page release form. They had twelve tons of equipment. When the leader of the group interviewed me about my experiences with ghosts I tried to explain about my depression, my drinking, and the visions of my father, who had died on the bathroom floor after being hacked to bits by oncologists for over a year. I told him I knew it was all in my fucked head.

The investigator said it sounded like a case of demonic possession and waved one of his little machines up and down my body. It squeaked and squonked and he and his team suggested a priest be brought in to "clear" both me and the house. When I balked he whispered to my wife that the force might have already taken too great a hold over me.

The more I suggested the whole thing was nonsense the more rooted they all became that I had devils. As a bipolar drunk screenwriter with a half-decade-long track record of alcoholism, drug addiction, mental ward stays and a string of failed films, I didn't exactly hold the high ground in the argument, so I let them do their thing.

The priest came in and blessed each room. He did a little baptism ceremony thing, splashing water in my face and asking me to follow the tenets of Jesus and renounce Satan. I said what I was supposed to say. I was Catholic, so I was doomed to listen and obey. My wife embraced the investigators afterward, and they said they were glad to help people like us in dire need.

After everybody left I tried to get sex off my old lady and she fled into the bathroom until I passed out after throwing back a pint of JD. She left me the next day. I hadn't seen her since.

So I was back in the bin. The straps were the worst part of the ordeal. I always reacted badly to them. I fought like a maniac to get free, never quite remembering that if I just acted calm for a little while the nurses would release me after a few questions and a pill or two. Instead, I pitted myself against the bonds, snarling and hissing and turning purple as I struggled. You'd think I would've learned by now.

I hoped I hadn't given up more intestine. My shoulders hurt, which meant I'd wrenched them out of the sockets and the docs had been forced to pop them back in. I could feel the tight pull of tape along my collarbone.

My mother sat at my bedside, surrounded by Grandma, Aunt Carmela, my older sister Debbie, my cousin Jane, my cousin Caroline, and a crying baby.

I wasn't sure which of them had brought the kid, but even in my state I wondered, how screwed up a mother did you have to be to bring a baby to the bin? I wasn't the only one in my family who had troubles.

I was cornered by live women and dead men. My grandmother's whispered prayers were something of a comfort. My mother and aunt discussed their recent dye jobs. My ma wasn't happy with hers but Aunt Carmela insisted it looked nice. Aunt Carmela hated her own, though, which my ma insisted looked fine. Debbie made no sound at all. She was mentally disabled. She could say simple words and she could laugh loudly and happily in a way that was either infectious or frightening, depending on the circumstances.

My cousin Caroline had married poor and looked as haggard as ever. My cousin Jane had married rich and looked as blessed and prosperous as usual. They talked together about the baby, if it needed feeding, if it needed changing. If I'd ever been told whose kid this was, I'd forgotten. If I'd ever met the kid before, I'd forgotten. I didn't know if it was a boy or a girl. It cooed and occasionally squawked, and I wondered how many nutjobs in this place were here because they'd murdered or stolen children.

I didn't recognize the ward. It must have been a new place, or at least a new wing. Sometimes they shuttled me around if I didn't snap out of it fast enough. The blackouts could last anywhere from a couple of days to a week. Once I went on a three-day binge and woke up without my wallet, glasses, or shoes at the Deer Park train station. I was stretched out across the tracks. Maybe I had done it to myself. Maybe someone was trying to get rid of evidence. About fifty morning commuters were staring down at me, waiting for the big finale to the show. When I climbed off the tracks there were groans of dismay. Everybody needed a little more excitement in their lives.

Grandma was dressed entirely in black. She'd been dressing that way for the last sixty years, since her husband had died of pneumonia in a freezing flat in Queens. The last ten, though, she'd had a small square of black crêpe pinned to her breast. That was for me. She held a white rosary in her lap and was saying her ten millionth prayer in my honor.

My mother knew I was awake. She stood and moved to my side. The others all started unfurling like geese. Ma had used half a tube of dark red lipstick and looked like she'd torn out someone's throat. If I had still been in the middle of the DTs, I would've been screaming at the sight of her.

My dad was smoking an unfiltered Camel, having learned nothing from his misery over the last year of his life. You'd think a dead man might act a little healthier than that. His mouth moved like he was talking but nothing came out. My guilt and shame liked to torment me with the my father's silence. It knew I'd give anything to hear his voice again.

He occasionally stabbed the air with his cigarette like he was emphasizing important points. Maybe these were the lessons of manhood I was supposed to have gotten thirty years ago. I tried to listen. I tried to concentrate. My cousin Jane asked what the hell I was looking at. My sister told her I was listening to my father. Deb knew me.

My father stood in a T-shirt, his powerful forearms so hairy that you could barely make out the faded tattoos he'd gotten in the Navy. When he was sixteen he'd lied about his age and joined the military to go fight and kill Japs. When I was sixteen I couldn't even find my dick.

I turned my head and caught a glance of my first great love, Kathy Lark, who'd vanished when we were ten. I've spent days on end searching for her in my writing and my dreams. I've walked along beaches and through woods and parks, wondering if I'd stumble across her grave or discover some cryptic message that would help me solve the grand riddle of my life.

Ma put her hand on the side of my face. She was a strong woman. All the women in my family were strong, much stronger than the men. I met her eyes. She grinned sadly. She wasn't angry. That meant I hadn't done anything too bad this time.

"Where am I?" I asked.

"Pilgrim," she said.

"I don't recognize the ward."

"It's in the back, the other building. They reopened it in the spring."

"I think I remember that."

There were five buildings to Pilgrim, some of them abandoned, some being rebuilt. As a teenager my friends and I and our girls would drive through the gaping holes in the wire fence and party on the grounds.

The others all shuffled into place, ringing the bed like Victorian doctors readying leeches. Debbie held the baby, talking gibberish. The kid giggled.

"How long, Ma?"

"Four days."

"I don't have the shakes."

"You weren't drunk. You just–"

"I don't need to know. Cops? Any charges?"

"Not so far as we know."

I let out a sigh of relief I hadn't realized I had been holding in. I didn't think I cared much about my life anymore, but every time I skirted some kind of trouble or tragedy I was happier than hell. "How long are they going to hold me?"

"You need to talk to the head psychiatrist, of course, but they should let you out in a week or two."

"Right. Thanks, Ma. My phone?"

"It's at home. Don't ask me to bring it. Half the reason you're in here is because of that goddamn phone."

It was probably true.

The others, staring down like the Inquisition, put their hands on me. Grandma held the rosary in front of my face and asked me to kiss it. I did. It brought tears to her eyes. She said, "You're a good boy, Tommy."

I was a lot of things, but I wasn't a good boy.

"What started you off this time?" Jane asked.

"I think my agent called to tell me my last script had been rejected by all the studios."

"You should be used to it by now," Caroline said. "Maybe it's time to do something else."

"Teaching," Jane suggested.

"You'd be a wonderful teacher," Aunt Carmela agreed, with light and hope in her voice.

I'd be a terrible teacher. Besides, what would I teach? I didn't know anything. I couldn't make a living. I'd had eight films produced as B and C grade films. I'd written twenty-five others. I'd left New York for Hollywood when I was nineteen. I'd garnered critical acknowledgment, studio success, money, and a beautiful wife, in that order. Then I'd had a run of flops. My bipolar manic-depressive split had gotten stuck on the downswing. We didn't have a pool boy, so my wife went after the neighbor's gardener. I cracked wide. I couldn't get the earth back under me. I'd returned to Long Island at thirty-five without a nickel, a woman, or a career. I'd been hibernating in my mother's basement for almost two years. I lived off the good graces of the ladies in my family.

It was amazing, really. When I set my mind to it I could compress the last twenty years into a paragraph. Maybe I could get a job writing obituaries.

"Tell the shrink I'm awake, would you?" I asked. "I want to talk to him and get the hell out of here."

Debbie put her hand on my chest. With her thick, grunting voice she said, "Love you."

Something inside me began to crack and loosen, and before I knew it the sob was already breaking free. As if I wasn't disgraced enough. I clamped my eyes shut, turned my head as far as I could, and pressed the side of my face into the mattress. I moaned like a maniac to drown out all other sound. For a while there were hands rubbing my back, soothing me. Then there weren't. My family left. I wept for at least an hour, lost inside my own fury and fantasies. Kathy leaned in and whispered my name. It kept the crying jag going. When I was finally through, I lay there sniveling, and even the deceased and the vanished were gone. I'd see them all again. At midnight, or in the shower, or the next time I made love, or at the last defeated moment of my death.

The new shrink wouldn't cut me loose until we hit all the bullet points of my life. She wasn't the standard pipe-smoking, sweater-wearing, beard-plucking, gray-haired head-plumber I'd dealt with many times before. I liked those fuckers. They got paid to nod. You said your piece and they quoted Freud, prescribed the sweet stuff, and sent you on your way.

This new one I had to deal with was a genuine believer. She felt it was a calling to help the psychotics, despondents, and the deranged back into society. Mine their depths, hold their secret traumas up to the sun, and vent the venom. She was fresh out of shrink school, maybe twenty-five, cute, with dimples and a beaming smile she only hit you with when you weren't looking at her full on. I could see her winding up with the wrong kind of neurotic and catching a sharpened pencil in the carotid.

So I laid it all out end to end, the way I had a dozen or more times before. She listened attentively, asking question after question, following the story of my life and seeking the unknowable pattern that I'd been seeking myself for thirty-five years. I told her about the ghosts. I told her about the priest. I told her about Kathy.

She asked, "Do you love her?"

"I was ten when she went missing."

"But do you love her?"

"I hardly knew her. She was just the girl who lived up the road."

"But do you love her?"

I'd written five movie scripts about little girls who'd gone lost. Only one had ever been made. In three of the screenplays, the child was found by the end. Twice alive, once not. A mountain of gravitas and lake of tears. In the other two scripts, she was never found at all. The burden of emptiness that never ended, questions forever unanswered. It could drive people crazy. It was one of those that had gotten funding and become something of an indie hit.

The shrink waited. My gaze wandered her office. It was freshly painted and well decorated. She knew she had asked a meaningful question. She was exceedingly proud of herself for it. Her dimples were on show. Her smile was at full wattage, so long as I didn't really look at her.

People might rightly assume that even after a quarter century Kathy Lark was still on my mind.

I wondered what the last thought was that had rushed through Tony Todesco's head the second before he spotted the grille of the car coming to kill him. Did he find the great theme of his life then, or was it merely the thunder strike of terror? Did he see his mother or God? Did he somehow picture me sitting here in this seat of pain thinking of him and Kathy? If I tried hard enough, could I send a signal backward through my life and tell him to get the hell off Old Miller Road?

I didn't love anyone else, so maybe I loved Kathy. She had the good grace to never become an adult, never break my heart, never leave me. She was everything I needed whenever I wanted it. She took my hand, she pressed her lips to that spot under my ear, she draped across my lap, and she gave me strength.

She was talking to me now, saying, "You could make this cutie pie shrink fall over for you, if you wanted her."

I didn't hear Kathy's voice. I couldn't even remember what she sounded like. Instead, I saw the words laid out across a computer screen, lines of dialogue from my next failed script. Sweat dappled my forehead. The urge to write was immense. My fingers burned, and my guts trembled with the need. It was almost sexual in nature. We all sought release. We all had to get off in our own ways. The nymphos greased each other's asses, the enraged broke their fists against one another's skulls, and my kind burned to filter the world through tiny black words on pages of white light.

She scratched out notes while I fought to keep from tearing the pen and pad out of her hands. I wanted to discuss her dimples. I thought I could describe a very poetic and moving love scene that wouldn't degrade into the perverse even when she got starkers and jumped me in my seat. She met my eyes once again.

"You don't feel comfortable answering the question?"

Which question was she fucking talking about? Didn't she understand I had dozens of questions ripping in and out of me every minute of the day? I still didn't know who had brought the baby into the bin. I still couldn't figure out how to sell another screenplay in Hollywood. I didn't know where my ex was, I didn't know why my mother's basement smelled like an autumn breeze blowing through the cemetery my father was buried in.

Tony, stay off Old Miller Road. Cut left, take Vincent Avenue instead. Listen to me, kid; hear me. You're in my head, aren't I in yours? The neighbors' kids had eaten ice cream, sitting on the red curb for weeks. I'd found a shard of busted bike reflector that I'd kept in my desk drawer for fifteen years... no, twenty, at least twenty... wait, maybe I still had it.

"Thomas?"

It was my name. She was calling my name from the end of a long tunnel. I could barely see her at the far end, just a shadow against the recesses of still greater shadows. Tunnels connected the five buildings that made up Pilgrim.

"Tommy?"

You heard stories about what happened down there. What the whackjobs did to each other, what the orderlies forced weak, ill women to do. I made up stories about what happened there. One of my produced films featured a scene shot under an overpass instead of in a tunnel, and they brought another screenwriter in to fuck with the arc, but they still went for blood. It was mine.

"Tom?"

"Yes?"

"Do you think you can answer the question?"

"Sure," I said. "No, I don't love Kathy. I was ten when she went missing."

I played along. I always did, eventually. I was a vanilla pudge, but I could be a charmer when I had to be. I responded well; I pretended interest and insight. I cried on cue, I quoted Rimbaud and Baudelaire, first in the original French, and then in translation. I started twelve-stepping. I promised amends to my higher power. I managed mystical breakthroughs. The cutie stared into my face and smiled. I got out.

I decided to walk home from Pilgrim State. The hospital was across the street from Suffolk Community College, where I'd spent two years getting a useless associate's degree. About a mile and a half farther on was the high school. I prowled the parking lot like a chicken hawk. I listened to the bell ring and the kids filling the halls and switching classrooms. I stood there so long that security came around in their little prowl car and threatened to call the cops. There was always a problem with Pilgrim patients wandering around the houses they'd grown up in, the schools they'd attended, the graves of their forefathers.

I quoted Rimbaud to the security guards and they pulled out their billy clubs. I took off across the football field where I'd never played a game or been a hero or laid a cheerleader. Clouds covered the sun. I broke into the woods at the edge of the field and made my way through a trail where we used to drink beer and talk of pussy and the future. The other end of the trail opened into an alley and backed onto a bodega where the salsa music rang out like it was already Saturday night.

I bought a bottle of cold water and sucked it down without taking a breath. Then I picked up a pint of bottom-shelf scotch. The Puerto Rican girl behind the counter, who was swinging her hips in sync with the beat, said, "I need to see your ID."

I was a little surprised, but not much. My mother had dyed my hair while I was in blackout, perhaps at my urging, perhaps not. My gray patch was gone. I was fat and pale enough that my face was free of wrinkles, and my glasses covered the crow's feet. I could pass for twenty if I never opened my mouth.

I showed her my ID. She couldn't hide her surprise that she was so off on my age. "Sorry," she said.

"Don't be, it's a compliment." I pulled a package of breath mints from beside the register and laid it on the counter. "These too."

She handed me the scotch and mints in a paper bag. I stood out in front of the store and sipped from the bottle and let the booze give me that sweet burn I loved so much for the first ten seconds and hated the rest of the time.

The shadow of a cross broke against the sky. St. Anne's church was half a mile down the road, practically across the street from the Holiday Twin. I had seen maybe five hundred movies at the Twin since I was a kid, many of them in the last year of my father's life, when he knew he was dying and made an effort to instill in me memories that would remain sharp throughout the fog of decades.

His own father had died when he was seven, the same age I was when they started cutting into him, leaving him with biopsy scabs and scars all across his chest and throat. In fourteen months he went from a strong, athletic, gravel-voiced foreman at Lockheed Martin to a hobbling, thin, shivering, hollow-faced phantom with a pervasive hack.

We went to the movies almost every evening, wildly inappropriate exploitation and horror flicks. The ushers gave him looks of curiosity and disgust. He bought tons of candy and we stuffed our faces. He laughed loudly in his seat whenever something hit him right. He didn't give a shit if he offended anyone. He was dying. He had three-quarters of one lung left. He was freer than he'd ever been before. It gave him a casual grace and comforting redemption.

I couldn't always follow what was happening on the screen. He took time to explain the ins and outs of the stories to me. He never let the shushers stop him. His coughing sent audience members out of the theater asking for their money back. He one time hacked so badly that he spit a piece of popcorn five or six rows into a black girl's afro. She confronted him and gave him hell for a minute, disregarding his apology, until she noticed the scars on his neck as if his throat had been cut ear to ear three or four times over. She ran back to her seat. She knew she'd been talking to a dead man.

After the movies we'd walk to St. Anne's, my old man limping badly, tired and spitting blood into his handkerchief, desperately wanting a cigarette despite them having already murdered him. I was a lapsed Catholic at seven. He taught me to pray. He showed me the power of icons, symbols, and ritual. We knelt together. We lit candles together. We sat in the pews in silence in an empty church and he muttered, breathless, "Don't forget me, Tommy."

"I'll never forget you, Daddy."

But he knew the truth. It made him weep. I rubbed his back, crying along with him, thinking I had done something wrong. He hugged me and kissed the top of my head and called me "baby." It made me cry harder.

His own father had tried to leave an impression on him as well, and hadn't been able to. He couldn't recall his father's face any more than I could remember my dad's now. Seven years old is just too young. The years pile on distractions, diversions, pain, and interference. He had wanted me to remember him and I had failed. I only remembered the scenes that I wrote out in screenplays, embellishing abundantly, with the faces of handsome popular actors playing us in my head.

I took another long pull on the scotch and stood in the middle of the road wondering if I should step left to the church or right to the movie theater. I couldn't make up my mind. If this were a scene in a movie—and they were all scenes in movies, the one running in my head, the one I was always writing no matter what I was doing—I would fall to my knees and a sad piano riff would rise up as the camera pulled back and left me in darkness.

Instead I stood there until the dramatic sweep was gone from my mind, and then I got the hell out of the street and walked to the theater. Learning to love shit films was my father's real legacy

Both flicks at the Twin were horror sequels. I knew the writers on both of them but had never seen either movie or any of the predecessors in the franchises. One series was about a mutant family of ghoulish gravediggers who solved crimes and saved town children despite their freakish appearances. The other was about a cop with an evil split personality that took over at night, and the cop chased him looking for clues without ever realizing he was hunting himself.

The theater was full. It was two in the afternoon and the place was packed with bitter-eyed unemployed men and teenagers ditching class. The kids could sense how close they were to becoming their own older brothers, uncles, and fathers. There wasn't even enough fight left in them to pretend to rebel with their politics, music, clothing, or hairstyles. We all sat out there in the dark, looking and acting the same. The films broke across our faces with the same self-indulgent, empty-headed hackneyed motives and consequences. We chuckled in the same places. We groaned at the strained believability, the wooden acting, the lack of denouement, the poor payoff. The music stingers didn't make any of us jump. Halfway through the second film I realized the scotch was gone and I was eating candy I hadn't bought.

The guy two seats to my left was watching me pluck chocolate-covered caramels from the box. I stopped, unsure of what to do. This was the kind of thing that drove men out of their heads, that made them fight to the death. He was going to head home to argue credit card percentages, bitch with his mortgage broker, scream at his wife, demand more from his kids. He couldn't even watch a bad movie without some asshole stealing his candy. He might wind up in Pilgrim chatting with the cutie pie, listening to her ask, "Did you love those chocolates?"

I gagged and swallowed, held the box back out to him.

I whispered, "I'm sorry."

"It's okay," he said. His voice was genuinely forgiving. He sounded a lot like how I remembered my father's voice to sound. Except I couldn't remember the sound of my father's voice, so everybody sounded like him. Even my mother, the paperboy, the schizo cop on the screen chasing his own tail. The movie was going to end with him arguing with the mirror. Half the fucking movies in Hollywood ended with somebody arguing with the mirror.

"I'll go get you another box at the concession," I said.

"Don't bother."

"It's no trouble at all."

"I wasn't liking them much anyway. You enjoyed them more than I did."

I reached for my wallet to pay him for the candy and he said harshly, almost breathlessly, "Don't pull your money out."

"But—"

"Just don't."

"Right."

Each flick had a ton of flashbacks, and whenever the music shifted and the film got supersaturated and fell into slow motion to show a shift in time, I felt myself rolling backward into my own flashbacks. They rose up before my eyes and covered whatever was happening on the screen.

I saw myself on the five-day bus ride to L.A., clutching my satchel full of scripts, three hundred bucks in my pocket, a Visa card, my shirt damp the first day with my mother's tears. Grandma had given me a holographic picture of the sacred heart of Jesus. You turned it one way and Christ was sort of giving a roguish glare, his arms wide open in loving ministration. Turn it aside and you saw the thorns tightening across his torn-out heart, blood dripping, pumping, arterial spray practically painting your face. You couldn't wish for better luck than that. I had kissed the card and slid it through my window just as we left Port Authority. It wouldn't go to waste. My grandmother's prayers would help someone even if they couldn't help me.

The cop flashed back to the early trauma that had fractured his psyche. He watched his mother having sex with strangers while his father, a member of S.W.A.T., stopped terrorists and saved kidnapped kids on out-of-control buses. The dad finally caught Mom doing the nasty with some skell, and Dad got on all his gear and got his machine gun and went shitstorm crazy out on the city streets, killing dozens of innocent people, including kids.

It was overcooked and half-baked at the same time. The screenwriter had a habit of peppering his films with wildly exaggerated and extraordinary events. Like you'd go more crazy if your father killed ninety-four people in midtown Manhattan instead of if he'd just slapped Mom around. Like he had to be a S.W.A.T. demolitions expert instead of just some donut-eating mook blue knight waiting his twenty-year pension out. Whenever the cop's evil self cut loose on the screen, I knew the actor was thinking, *Oscar time, baby.*

I sat there eating another guy's candy, watching the cop talking into the mirror, the mirror sneering back at him. I knew the words that would come out of each of his two mouths.

You stay away from my beautiful daughter, Becky Lee!

She's not your daughter! She's... mine!

Nooooo!

Right cross into mirror, shattering the glass.

Wife runs in, *What happened? How did you cut yourself?*

It's nothing, I'm fine.

Daddy, Daddy, you're bleeding!

Oh, Becky Lee. Oh, Becky Lee!

I sucked the caramels down. I didn't find solace in food. I didn't find love. But I found something. And I ate like a starved pig working his way through the truffle patch, a hog gone razorback wild for the taste of meat. Oh, Becky Lee, you little bitch, you stupid plot device, you fifteen-year-old oversexed chippie with lissome curves and pliant tits and an ass I'd kill half a nation for.

Gossip had it that the actress playing Becky Lee had been to Planned Parenthood twice in the past year already. She'd become pregnant by the actor playing her father, the cop. I looked at his ten-foot black eyes on the screen and guessed it was true. I had an evil side too. I wanted to sneak up behind him and get him in a headlock and hold him there while he struggled weakly, while he wilted, turning blue and then purple. I'd let him sip a bit of air before I laid him out on the bedroom carpet, then slipped up step by step on little Becky Lee. Ready to eat her candy. Oh, Becky Lee!

The theater was empty. The screen was blank. The show was over and everybody had already left, but I hadn't noticed. I was sweaty and gasping. My chest hurt as if I'd taken a couple of left hooks to the ribs. I reached up and touched my mouth. My lips were twisted and frozen into a hateful grin.

"Jesus," I whispered, just to get them working again.

Dad, you never should've taken me to the movies. It wasn't your fault, as you coughed up your smoke-soaked lungs, but you shouldn't have done it.

I was nearly home when I decided I didn't want to go there, but by then it was too late. I chewed the mints to hide my whiskey breath. My mother was perched in the bay window, staring at the neighbors, watching the world go by. She saw me come around the corner and hesitate. If she'd only taken a bathroom break maybe I would've run. Except there was nowhere to run to.

I crossed the lawn with what I hoped looked like a buoyant stride. I smiled and waved. She looked at me like she saw her own death approaching. My mother was nearly seventy and didn't need any more of my shit in her life.

Deb met me at the door on the fly. She hit me low and hard like a halfback going for the sweet spot, and I nearly went backward over the porch rail. I'd forgotten just how powerful my sister was. She hefted me into her arms and grunted a few words I couldn't understand. I patted her back and held her to me. She smiled, turned, and was back inside in a flash.

When she wasn't at school, Deb sat in front of the TV with a little fold-out table playing solitaire, watching Lawrence Welk and game show reruns from the 70s. Sometimes with Grandma, sometimes alone when our grandmother was out at the bingo parlor or getting her hair done up in a pink rinse.

I stepped in. The house sighed my name. The ghost chasers had gone to the wrong place. If there were any supernatural forces trying to drag me across the veil, they were here. Your angels, demons, and phantoms might be savage, benevolent, or just hungry for your blood, but one thing was for certain, they've always always always been with you.

The muted cries of game show audiences. The careful snapping of cards.

My mother was in the kitchen. She was usually in the kitchen. Either cooking or reading the paper or leaning forward propped over a kitchen chair, facing the door, waiting for me. Or waiting for the cops to bring news that I was paralyzed or dead. The same way she'd done when I was fifteen. She was the only person in America who still had a land line. A bone-white phone that matched the walls, with an actual tangled cord. It reminded me that I had to call my agent.

My mother said, "Are you hungry? I've got leftover baked ziti in the fridge."

My ma. My ma was built solid, a fireplug of a woman, wide in the hips, with hands that had thickened over the years and looked like they could tear the heads off chickens. She'd started as a typist for a New York paper when she was fifteen and spent more than fifty years killing keypads. She was so fast that the air around the old metal keys would superheat and brown the pages. I was fast too, on my laptop, but nothing like her.

My ma, who'd survived it all, who'd buried her husband, who'd had to raise a mentally handicapped daughter mostly on her own, who'd been forced to deal with my troubles from day one. I'd started drinking early, binging, not because I wanted to get drunk but because the words so often didn't want to come. I'd stare at that old Underwood and try to will myself to become a part of the overwhelming grandeur of literature. I was a teenager without a story to tell. I banged out sentences about Kathy Lark. I made up histories of lives I had not lived. I wrote novels that were four pages long. I stole bourbon from the liquor cabinet and woke up in the shower with my clothes on, my mother screaming outside the bathroom door, "Why? Why? Why are you doing this?"

I'd type: You made your mother cry today.

My ma; the soundtrack to her life is Lawrence Welk playing on a tin box in a distant room, cards shuffling, Debbie occasionally mumbling responses to the game show questions. She calls out vowels. She laughs when the audience laughs, unsure of why. Grandma sometimes yells to my mother in Italian. My mother always responds in English, wearily. Somehow, the weight of their dialogues centers me, grounds me. I can almost pretend I know another language. I can picture myself on the streets of Sicily, wearing a fedora, walking through the plaza with soulful eyes and a languid smile.

My ma. I used to send her home money when I was doing well. I was never a big gun, but when there was some extra, I mailed checks home. It wasn't because I wanted to help her out. It was because I needed to prove to myself what a wonderful son I was, what a fine human being. Over ten years I sent her maybe 40K. It wasn't much. It wasn't enough. It should've been more. It didn't matter. She never spent a penny of it. She put it in a bank account with my name on it. My ma, she had known the bottom would eventually drop out. When it did, my ex took everything. She deserved it. I didn't want it. I had no use for a love seat. I couldn't afford the last month down and the security deposit. I called my ma and she answered that very phone on the wall, and I chumped out and asked her for a few bucks. She sent all forty large back plus interest to make my defeat complete.

The money kept me going while the scripts were being passed around with no takers. The cash ran out fast even in a two-room apartment in East Hollywood. My ma, she explained that I could always come home again. My old bedroom had been turned into Grandma's sewing room, but half the basement was still free. I just had to dump the dehumidifier tank and clean out the filter once a week.

If only she'd taken a world cruise with the cash. If only she'd bought herself a bright-eyed cabana boy.

"So?" she asked.

"Hm?"

"Are you hungry?"

I didn't answer. No answer was usually the right answer. She went to the fridge and got out the plastic bowl of ziti and heated it up. She made some antipasto and a small salad with oil and vinegar dressing. I ate better at home than I had over the last ten years and I still lost twenty pounds.

I sat at the kitchen table. Grandma's sewing machine was whirring away. One of those old-fashioned ones with the foot pedal and the big-ass spools of thread that spun like mad when she really got going. She had about five hundred pounds of yarn stacked in there for all her crocheting. Every color you could imagine and some that didn't seem like they should fit on the spectrum. There were dozens of thick, well-crafted blankets all over the house.

I was hungry. Sometimes it felt like I'd never be hungry again, but suddenly I was famished. I ate the salad and the antipasto and had to control myself from licking at crumbs. My mother served me the ziti. I sat in the chair I had sat in all during my youth. She offered me the grating cheese, and without my saying a word she sprinkled exactly the right amount across the plate. I tore in.

When I finished she cleared the plates away as she had done ten thousand times before.

"Who brought a kid?" I asked.

"What kid?"

"The kid."

She looked at me the way she sometimes did, as if I were speaking in code and she needed a couple of seconds to decipher it.

She cocked her chin and said, "What do you mean?"

"Which one of them brought a baby to the bin?"

"The bin?"

"The hospital. Did Caroline or Jane bring the kid to the hospital?"

"Whose baby?" she asked.

"That's what I'm asking. Whose baby?"

Grandma walked in and hugged me. She looked at my empty plate and said to my ma, "*Alimentare il vostro figlio!*"

"I did feed him," my mother said. "You think I wouldn't feed my son?"

Grandma kissed me on the head. She wanted to ask questions, or offer up support, or reach inside my chest and draw out the weight of my sins so she could carry them herself. She wanted to tell me that life wasn't so bad, that with patience came happiness. But what kind of faith could you put in a woman who's been in mourning for forty years?

Instead she just kissed me again on the crown, then walked into the living room and sat down with Debbie to watch Welk.

Tom Piccirilli

My mother turned away to the sink and started washing the dishes.

I went to the basement. My phone was on the nightstand. I had forty-two voice mail messages. Some of them would be from former friends and lovers I'd called during my drunken rage, telling me to drop dead. At least ten of them would be from my agent, Monty Stobbs, promising fortune and success and asking to borrow money. No matter how many times my screenplays were rejected, he never lost the faith. He never lost the faith because he never had any in the first place. He didn't read my scripts. He didn't read the reviews of my movies. He was smarter than that. I played the first message and heard my own voice.

I told myself, "If you're listening to this it means you struck out again. Why can't you ever do the goddamn job right?"

I almost answered. I almost said, I don't know. I just don't know. But don't blame me. You fouled it too. You botched it just as badly as I did. Why did you call me instead of just jumping off the big ledge?

I tossed the phone aside. The ziti wasn't sitting well with the scotch, the caramels, and the mints. I shuddered, ran for the small unfinished bathroom, and threw it all up.

I sat in front of my laptop and turned it on. I listened to the creaking floor above me, my ma, my poor ma, wondering what her life meant, what kind of grace she'd receive in paradise for being put through all of this. For forty g's she could've bought a sailboat and disappeared to Tahiti.

The fucking polkas kept filtering down.

I wrote:

```
FADE IN:

A man, thirty-seven, sits in front of his lap-
top, seated in his mother's basement. This is
TOMMY. He stares emptily at the screen. On it
are the words: FADE IN. He writes nothing more.
He waits. He thinks about a spider monkey.
```

WHAT MAKES YOU DIE

Sometimes the low point of your life doesn't come when you're lying in the gutter smelling like the bottom of a bottle of scotch, or when your wife finally leaves you, or when you crap out for the last time at a casino and realize you've gambled away your kid's college fund.

Mine came at a Christmas party in Beverly Hills, thrown by a rich producer much younger than me, attended by beautiful, high-powered movers much younger than me, and whose guest of honor was a screenwriter much younger and much more successful than me.

I was caught halfway between wanting to drown myself in the pool, which was the size of a lake, or the hot tub, which was the size of an Olympic pool.

I'd spent most of my career writing scripts about Zypho, an alien critter from "beyond the edge of space" that used its tentacles to suck out either brain or vaginal juices, depending on what market Monty's backers were attempting to hit. I'd seen Zypho lopped down to a G-rated kiddie show in Japan, and it was also a hit on the adult market thanks to a few clumsily inserted full-penetration scenes. With a hand-held camera Monty had managed to tune the flick up to triple-X stature that appealed to the kink crowd. Tentacles or rubber dildos, nobody really gave a shit so long as they went in the right, or even the wrong, slot.

The only reason I was at the party was because Monty Stobbs thought it would be good for us to rub elbows with the new Hollywood elite. The Hollywood elite changed about every six months, and we were about nine changeovers behind. He said the rich producer owed him one from some minor hit they'd worked on together years before, but it wasn't until we arrived that I realized we'd actually crashed the party. Luckily, it would have been too gauche and provincial for them to throw us out on Christmas Eve.

The only elbow-rubbing I was doing was when I had to push my way through the crowd while the wealthy kids stared at me in confusion, wondering how someone with a streak of gray in his hair wasn't using a walker. I orbited various groups of celebrity actors and musicians, keying in on vacuous conversations punctuated with well-practiced titters and giggles and hyped by hard liquor, crank, and heroin. It seemed that H was back in style. What was old always became new.

Some of the folks I'd worked with before. Some of them recognized me. Those who did moved to the other side of the room. I didn't blame them. That's how the town worked. You caught failure the same way you picked up herpes. You got too fucking close.

Some of them were dressed up like elves or wearing Santa costumes. They were beginning to organize a wet T-shirt contest out by the pool that looked like a lake, so I had to forestall my plans for drowning myself there. I turned to the hot tub and there were twelve people up to their necks in the bubbling waters. They were trying to stare lustfully at one another except they were all thrown off by a spider monkey clinging to the towel rack.

If I had my druthers, I wouldn't want to screw anybody in sight of a spider monkey either. But then again, I was thirty-five years old at the time and I'd never had my druthers. I wasn't certain what a druther was, but the lack of it added to my funk.

At around midnight the growing group sexual tension of the party was beginning to reach critical mass. Twice I'd been asked if I had any crank or heroin, and twice I'd been asked to bring the lady a wine spritzer. I was feeling under-dressed, which was ironic seeing as how people were beginning to disrobe, and those who weren't getting naked were wearing elf outfits. I hadn't seen Monty for over an hour.

Despite my fear that there might be more animals indigenous to the South American rain forests about the place, I started trying doors, looking for a way out. I thought I would crack Monty in the mouth and thumb a ride home to my squalid pad in East Hollywood. I was drunk and starting to feel crazy. I had the capacity to hurt someone.

Finally, I opened a door and there my agent was. The man in charge of my career, my finances, my life.

"Holy Christ!" I shouted.

"Help me!" Monty screamed.

Someone with a serious mad on had done ole Monty wrong. He was handcuffed wrist and ankle to the four-poster bed. He was dressed up like Rudolph, replete with rubber red ball nose and reindeer antlers with a tightened chin strap to hold them in place. There were trailing reins tied down over his chest and a collar with big jingly bells on it. He even had these booties on that looked like hooves.

"I've got to admit, Monty," I told him, "I was feeling a little low tonight, but you've perked me right up."

"Get me out of here!"

"What the hell happened?"

"You remember the girl I was with?"

"No."

"Well, apparently she's a screenwriter, sent me something once and I rejected it."

"You've never rejected anything in your career, Monty. You don't read anything. You accept everything. You steal what you can. What's the real story?"

"I guess I tried to make her last year at this same party. She says I groped her and she threw wine in my face."

"And you don't remember?"

"You know how many women have thrown wine in my face?"

I tugged at the high-tensile steel chains around his left ankle. "So she was waiting for you this year? She even brought four sets of handcuffs. And these booties! You must've really pissed that lady off."

"All you fucking writers are too sensitive."

The bed was a massive metal four-poster with welded joints. The headboard was as solid as the grille on a '57 Chevy. I made a halfhearted effort for a couple of minutes. "No way, Monty."

"Goddammit! Okay, okay, then listen. You've got to go get a hacksaw."

"Where am I going to get a hacksaw in Beverly Hills on Christmas Eve?"

"You're right. You've got to go get the key from her. You've got to apologize for me."

"What's her name?"

"I don't know. I wasn't thinking long term."

Only Monty would think that asking a woman's name might be considered a long-term relationship. "What's she look like?"

"Raven hair, a nice rack."

"There's about four hundred hotties like that out there."

"I know, I know! Ah, well... she's got a sharp look about her. Thoughtful. I don't know, just go look for her!"

I started to shut the door and he screamed, "Wait! Come take this shit off my head!"

"No," I told him. "You're right, we writers are too sensitive. You're getting off easy. I was ready to break your jaw for dragging me to this party and grinding down what little ego I have left. Sit tight, and don't make too much noise. There's a spider monkey roaming around that will come and eat your eyes out."

I slammed the door before he could say anything more.

The party crowd had somehow doubled since midnight, and they were singing "Let it Snow." What I would've given to be walking around Rockefeller Center in Manhattan and watching the ice skaters.

The first two points were easy enough to check off so far as Monty's lady was concerned. Raven hair and a nice rack. The thoughtful expression was a little more difficult to find. It took me a while.

She was standing off alone from the crowd, and there was a tinge of sadness to her eyes. Monty would mistake that for thoughtfulness. Even if I hadn't already fallen in love with her for dressing Monty up like Rudolph, I thought the melancholy gaze could drive me the rest of the way. In an instant of sudden, immense clarity I knew I had to have her, and I wouldn't be able to get her, and I would wind up home in my mother's basement slowly going out of my tree.

Monty's girl was dressed in a demure red dress that made me think of a sexy Mrs. Kringle. The black hair was cut into soft waves that framed her lovely heart-shaped face. She wasn't quite smiling and wasn't quite grinning, and yet she appeared to be amused by all that was going on around her. She appeared to be drinking a cosmo. She seemed about as out of place as I was. She was a writer. That meant she was at least halfway to crazy already.

I walked up and asked, "You wouldn't happen to have the key to four handcuffs, would you?"

"That's got to be the worst opening line I've ever heard," she said.

"Under normal circumstances, I'd agree with you."

She sipped her cosmopolitan and gave me those eyes again. "Is that prick a friend of yours?"

"Agents don't have friends, only clients."

"Is he thinking of pressing charges?"

"It would be your word against his, which is why he's lost every court case he's ever been involved in. I doubt he'd want this one to go before a jury."

"I know you," she said. "I mean, I think I've seen some of your work. You do the Zypho movies, don't you?"

"I started off trying to win an Academy Award, but somewhere along the way I downgraded to writing about a brainsucking critter from beyond space."

"You're still alive. In this town, that counts for something."

It counted in any town and every town, but I didn't know what it counted toward. The money I'd sent to my mother that she'd sent back to me years later was already gone. I was still alive but I was about to make a run for it, back to New York, back to my ma. My ex always called me a mama's boy. My ex called me a lot of things.

"Oh yeah," I said, "where'd you get those little booties?"

"At a sex shop on Rodeo."

"Jesus Christ, people actually wear them during sex?"

"I don't understand it either."

"Did you bring them specifically for Monty?"

"Him or four or five other guys."

"You've really have had it rough, haven't you?"

It brought the sorrow and anger out in full bloom. I liked seeing it. I wanted to know I wasn't the only one who'd been fucked by this town. I knew in my heart that ninety-nine percent of those kids who came in on buses like I had never accomplished nearly as much as I had, but it didn't do the rage eating me away any good. I liked seeing others beaten like I was beaten. I had no sympathy left. I couldn't afford it.

"Are you in a rush to get back to him?" she asked.

"Hell no, I'm only now starting to get my eyesight back. It was quite a scene in there."

She sipped her drink. I could smell somebody lighting up some meth. I wondered how many of the beautiful ones would be dead by next Christmas.

"You don't belong here either," she said.

"No. What's your name?"

"Trudy."

"Hello, Trudy. I'm Tommy Pic."

I took her hand. I didn't want to let go. I wanted to hold the side of my face to her palm. I wanted to recite French poetry to her.

She immediately rattled off the titles to three ultra-low-budget horror flicks I'd written for Monty. They'd all started out as serious explorations on the nature of relationships in the modern world and somehow ended up full of big-titted scream queens being chased through haunted houses in their skivvies. She tried to find something nice to say about my work but couldn't quite do it. I gave her points for trying.

"Come on," she said. "I can't breathe in here."

She led me out to the yard, beyond the pool, and then beyond a group of drunken revelers playing volleyball with water-filled condom, and even beyond the minor celebrity actress entwined with the minor celebrity director who'd passed out on a chaise lounge about six seconds before actual coitus. If the spider monkey went after the director's peeled banana he was going to wake up mighty damn quick.

Trudy and I wandered the estate and discussed writing and the vagaries of Los Angeles, and our general disappointments and occasional triumphs. At the end of our litanies we sort of fell into each other, at first just hugging very tightly before we worked toward a kiss.

It was soft and a little painful and altogether enchanting. The warm wind blew across our bodies, and when I kissed her again I felt a drop of sweat slide from her forehead and against my lips.

"I want you," she said.

"Even without the hoof booties or the little red nose?"

"Especially without those."

"Well, okay then."

It brought a soft, throaty chuckle out of her that worked itself into me until I was hard and needy. We lay in the grass and she waited for me to yank up her dress, but instead I leaned forward. We'd all been used by this damn town, and I wanted to be certain she wouldn't feel used by me now. She pressed her palm to my chest and dug her fingernails in and seemed a bit surprised that I was made of flesh and not film stock. I could see that Monty hadn't been the only bastard she'd run into.

The animal urge was there, but we took it gently, at first, and let the heat burn us wildly. She liked to kiss passionately. So did I. She was the first woman I'd been with since my ex.

I liked the feel of her skin. I grabbed her hair and held her to me. I tried to do it in a loving way but it's just not possible. I was starting to lose myself, which rarely occurred during sex, but she made it happen.

It was a gift, a rarity. She groaned deeply and again, and I realized she was saying my name. It was a very strange reassertion of my existence.

The things that could drive you out of your head. I plunged and kept my pacing slow so she'd know I meant every motion. We all need affirmation. Trudy moaned and the sweat streamed across her face. She kept her eyes open and locked on mine. "Don't close your eyes," she said.

"I won't."

"Look at me," she groaned.

"I will."

We were both covered in grass stains and breathing heavily as the wind blew hotter and hotter around us. My sweat splashed across her and she raised her hands to dig into my chest again. I liked the honest feel of her nails.

We kept our eyes open. She was on the edge and so was I. We stayed there for longer than either of us thought possible.

I dropped forward and drew her onto her side with me. We relaxed like that for a long time and gently stroked each other. I didn't know that a year later to the day I would stick a steak knife in my gut and cleave off four feet of intestine.

It took us a while to unwrap ourselves and get dressed again, and when we did we walked with our arms wrapped tightly around each other's waist as if trying to hold on to some lost hope that had been restored. Maybe only for the night.

"We still need to go let Monty loose," I said.

She didn't have a handbag and I could attest to the fact that she had no key on her. "They're trick cuffs. There's a tiny switch on them. You just have to press it."

"Cup your hand and pretend there's a key or he'll lose his mind."

When we got back to the house it took me three tries to find the right room.

I opened the door and saw the spider monkey was perched on Monty's head like Zypho trying to suck out brain juices, holding onto an antler in one hand and gripping a tuft of Monty's hair in the other. Monty had his eyelids scrunched tight in terror.

"It's been on my head like it's sitting on an egg!" he screamed.

WHAT MAKES YOU DIE

I leaned over and the monkey made a soft noise and jumped into my arms. Monty tentatively opened his eyes. He'd lost feeling in his limbs and it took him a few minutes to get his circulation going again. Trudy pretended to use a key to open the four sets of cuffs.

"Where's my clothes?" he asked.

"I threw them out the window," Trudy said.

"You," he said. "You...!"

Trudy smiled at him. "But don't bother looking down there, I think somebody stole them."

"You...!"

"Don't be nasty, Monty," I said. "It's Christmas Day. The only reason Scrooge didn't die alone and unloved was because he learned his lesson."

"Oh, fuck you people!"

He tore off the antlers and the plastic red nose, but the reins and the collar were heavy with buckles and straps and Monty didn't have enough feeling in his hands yet to work them.

It was almost 4:00 a.m. and the temperature had broken ninety. Rudolph pranced across the wide lawn and hopped into the back of his BMW. Trudy got in the passenger side and I got in and drove.

In New York, I thought, they're probably inside their apartments waking up with their trees and their presents, staring out at a blizzard, promising their kids a morning sled race in the park. Trudy took my hand and started singing "Let it Snow," and I put the air conditioner on full blast until Monty was shivering so hard his collar jangled in tune with the song.

We dropped her off. She made no promises. She said nothing more. She didn't take my number. I said something moderately desperate. She looked at me with the same sad eyes. I'd failed her by opening my mouth and proving my need. That wasn't how L.A. worked.

"What did she say her name was?" he asked.

"Trudy."

"Last name?"

"She never said."

"She played you. Nobody's actually named Trudy."

I knew that already.

After a couple of fitful hours of overheated sleep, I got up and broke my lease, sold my car, and climbed onto a bus headed back home to my ma's basement.

Like me, Monty had been chased out of L.A. Six months after I dragged my ass out of town, he followed. The movies weren't working out. He was giving New York television and theater a go. He'd become an "entertainment agency." I wasn't exactly sure what that entailed, but I knew he now repped stand-up comedians, jugglers, dog acts, Korean acrobats, and a one-man oom-pah-pah band. In addition to the average struggling New York actors looking for a guest spot on any of the Law & Orders or a chance to try out for the cast of Saturday Night Live. Monty didn't have any shame. It's why he was a survivor. It's also why I needed him.

For some reason I wound up with a little more respect for Monty after the spider monkey episode. Maybe I was just thankful to have had a moment when I'd been able to have a minor adventure at his expense. I'd also finally realized I wasn't cut out for the West Coast no matter how hard I worked to put off the inevitable.

I took the LIRR into the city. I climbed out at Penn and then took the C to West 4th and Sixth Avenue. Monty's office was in the West Village bookended between a magic shop and a family-owned Vietnamese restaurant where everybody scurried around and screamed at each other like they were about to launch the Tet Offensive all over again.

The magic shop didn't sell tricks like disappearing ink or top hats with bunnies, but instead was a place where you could actually find items for rituals of witchcraft. It was called Weird Sisters. I hadn't finished high school or attended college but I still got the reference. The three witches in Macbeth were named "the weird sisters."

There was no elevator in Monty's building and his office was on the fifth floor. I took the stairs and passed a clown in full makeup, big shoes, red ball nose, wacky wig — the complete outfit — muttering to himself on his way down. He didn't say anything, but he squeezed a variety of horns very bitterly. They played a furious and hateful song. Another of Monty's satisfied clients. I figured he was booking kids' birthday parties now too.

Monty had an elderly assistant named Glory Greer, who I thought might actually be Monty's Aunt Loretta brought down from Poughkeepsie. Glory was one of those women who put on half a tube of lipstick every day and mostly got it on her teeth. She wore her hair up in a huge modified bun that looked like a platypus lying on top of its eggs. A set of fake pearls hung quaintly around her neck. She always wore a gingham dress with a brightly colored bow at the top, and a sweater with three-quarter sleeves and only the top button buttoned. Glory wore a perpetually bright smile that was tinged with a touch of confusion. Behind her oversized glasses she offered a puzzled squint. I liked her because she seemed to have been kidnapped in the night a couple of years ago and still didn't know where she was or how she could ever get home again.

"Let me see if he's in," she said.

"He's always in. Where else does he have to go? In L.A. he could crash parties. Here they've got doormen."

"He could be taking a meeting."

"He just took one with some clown, and the clown didn't seem happy about the outcome."

Glory shook her head sadly. "Bango is an angry clown. That's his thing. He hits people in the face with his shoes."

"At kids' parties?"

"Political rallies, mostly."

"Does he get hired a lot?"

"He's got some lawsuits he's currently involved in. He broke some poor man's nose a number of weeks ago."

I felt for Bango. I understood his shtick. It probably started off as a genuine crowd-pleaser, running up to somebody and hitting him with an oversized padded shoe. But as time wore on, and the padding wore down, and his nerves tightened, and his makeup began to ruin his skin and stick in his crow's feet, Bango probably took more and more pleasure out of feeling his heels smashing someone in the teeth, payback motherfuckers, here's my contribution to your cause.

I pushed open the door to Monty's office. The place smelled of Vietnamese food. Monty liked to order from next door. The seventeen-year-old daughter of the owners made the deliveries. When Monty wasn't dressed for spider monkey lovin' he liked to ogle the Asian cuties.

"Where've you been? I've been calling for weeks."

It didn't matter what I told Monty. He never heard a word I said. I'd explain to him about the hospital and the blackouts and the depression, and he'd ask, "So, you rewrite that script yet? You need big tits in the third act." He also repped some ex-porn stars who wanted to recreate themselves as serious actresses. He booked them into soft core romantic thrillers where they simulated oral sex instead of doing the real thing. This seemed to satisfy them as ingénues and allowed Monty to brim with a certain kind of self-righteousness, like he was helping women to earn back their hard-fought self-respect. Maybe he was. They were also apparently willing to join in with the hot tub orgies if Monty had enough crystal meth on him.

He understood a lot about this world, but he'd never fully grasped the concept of the imperative creative impulse. He put it to use, and he made his 15 percent off of it, but he'd never totally get it.

But neither would I. If I could ever figure out why I felt the need to write scripts instead of just getting a job in a factory somewhere in Jersey, making tires or stamping sheet metal or baking dog biscuits, I would. Nothing was worse than describing scenes that would never be shot,

writing dialogue that would never be spoken. My ma down-
loaded streaming video onto her HDTV and would say,
"This movie is awful. Why would they make this *stronzo*
instead of something you wrote?"

And I would stare at her with the only expression I
could ever muster. The one that said, I don't know, Ma, I
just don't know. And behind me would rise the luxuriant
music of Lawrence Welk, and my sister would snap her
cards, six of hearts, three of clubs, jack of spades, and I'd
retreat to the basement again, thinking,

CLOSE-UP:

Push in on TOMMY PIC. He stands in his agent,
MONTY STOBB's, office. There's a twinkle of
deranged hope in his eyes. Despite all he
knows of the business he still somehow manages
to dream that he may yet find success. He
presses a hand to his belly, as if he feels a
deep-set infection in the lengthy, thick scars
creasing it.

"Well?" Monty asked.

"I've been busy."

"Working on something new?"

"Always."

"Your dedication has always impressed me."

"My ass."

"No, it's true. You remind me of me—"

"Now you're just being mean."

"—no matter what happens, you still keep working. Unlike
me, you don't always make money at it, but you're always
driven to keep moving forward. The words roll on. What's the
new one about?"

It didn't matter what I said. Monty always asked after
the new one. If the setup didn't involve a hot chick, his eyes
glazed over and I knew he was thinking about some other

Tom Piccirilli

client. Bango, or a soft-core pornie chick, or another screenwriter who was blasting out episodes of New York cop
shows. He still flew back to L.A. at least a couple times a
month to push movies at his third-string producer cronies.
He was right about one thing: he was always working and
always bringing in the bread.

"What did you want to see me about, Monty?"

"About the new one."

"Which new one?"

"Your new one. *What Makes You Die.* I like it. There's
something special about it. Special the way your early ones
were, the ones that made the big guns perk up. There's
some strong roles there, the kind that anyone on their way
up or on their way down would want to play. I think we can
move it. We might have a real moneymaker here. But I need
you sober and clear-headed. Will you have more finished
by, say, next Monday? I'll set up some meetings. We'll hit
the coast early in the week, visit some of our old friends, see
what we can get cooking."

I just stared at him. I didn't know what the hell he was
walking about. The last screenplay I'd finished had been titled
Every Shallow Cut. It was about a writer and his bulldog cross-
ing America trying to figure out some purpose to life. Monty
hated it. It was too esoteric. He liked the dog. He thought it
should be a comedy, where the dog drives and has a celebrity
voice. He suggested an actor who'd been dead over a year. I
didn't have the heart to tell him the guy was toes up.

Monty handed me some pages. I saw my name under a
title: *What Makes You Die.* Monty had taken the time to write
some notes. He never did that. I looked from the script back to
him. He said, "If you can work in some tits, fine. If not, well,
okay. But you've got to at least finish the second act. I can't
pitch only thirty-five minutes of a movie, Tommy. You've got
to give me more."

I flipped through the screenplay but couldn't seem to focus.
My gaze skittered off the pages. I saw words but couldn't string

them together. What I did make out seemed to be formatted the way I usually formatted scripts, in the font that I preferred. I spotted my name on the title page, my address, my cell phone number. It seemed to be mine. I didn't recall writing it. I had no idea how Monty had gotten it.

My vision was bright white and kaleidoscopic at the edges, a sure sign that an ocular migraine was about to hit. I desperately wanted a drink. Monty kept a bottle of scotch in his filing cabinet and I thought about making a dive for it. But he was looking at me in a way that he hadn't looked at me in years. I recognized it as optimism. He wasn't looking at me like he usually did, like I was dead but just hadn't fallen down yet.

"When did you get this?" I asked.

"When did I get it? What do you mean? I got it when you emailed it to me a week ago."

I'd been in the bin a week ago. They didn't allow cell phones or computer access.

"So?" he asked.

"So what?"

"So when can you have the rest of it done? I need a second act by next Monday. Can you make it?"

I looked at him, grinned, and said, "Sure."

I walked southeast across the city. I didn't know where I was going. I read Monty's notes as I walked and found his comments cryptic as hell. WHY IS THE GIRL IN THE BOX AND NOT IN THE BOWL? I THINK YOU SHOULD CLARIFY THE ROLE OF THE MEMENTO THIEF. IS IT A'S FATHER OR B'S BROTHER? WHEN DID HIS LEG GET CUT OFF AND IS IT THE SAME LEG IN THE BATHTUB? WHO LEFT THE OLD LADY'S CORPSE ON THE ROOF?

"The fuck?" I said.

The migraine was burning through my head. There was no pain at all, just wild psychedelic patterns of light corrupting my eyesight. I occasionally walked into people. It didn't matter much, this was New York, the street traffic was always clipping shoulders and giving each other flats. I couldn't catch my breath. I tried to find a bench to sit down on but there was nothing. I needed darkness and a drink to help my head. I kept going.

I found a bar next door to an artsy two-theater movie house. I didn't recognize the title of either film on the marquee. They sounded like documentaries. *Gift of My Father's Heart* started in ten minutes, *The Ruin of Dog Paradise* in fifteen. I swung into the bar and ordered a triple Jameson with a beer back. After I paid I saw that I had twenty-eight dollars left. My mother always stuffed a few bills into my wallet to help me get by. It shamed me and made me want to kill myself, but she was right, it also helped me to get by.

I emptied the short glass and the mug in ten seconds flat. It was the way I always drank. I hated the taste but enjoyed the effect. The heat ran down into my chest and stuck a red-hot pin in my heart. I winced and gritted my teeth against the pain. In a minute all my muscles began to loosen and a knot of barbed wire at the back of my head began to untangle.

The alcohol started to take the edge off. My vision began to clear a little. I read more of Monty's notes. I REALLY LIKE THE OLD MAN WITH ONLY HALF A FACE AND THE SHOTGUN. BRING HIM BACK IN FOR THE THIRD ACT. HIS DAUGHTER HAS BIG TITS, RIGHT? WHO KILLED THE MOUSE? IS THE MEMENTO THIEF IN THE HOUSE? DOES A'S FATHER HELP HIM ESCAPE FROM THE SICK NEIGHBOR? GREAT TENSION BETWEEN THE KID AND THE GUY WITH THE SHOVEL.

The bartender walked past and I pressed both my empty glass and mug forward, and said, "Another."

He gave me a refill of the Jameson's and some sweet microbrew. I threw the second triple shot down fast and followed it with the beer in four gulps. My stomach tumbled. The needle went all the way through my chest. I started to feel in control. I was eager to see the documentaries, but when I left the bar I finally noticed that the theater had been boarded over. It gave me a feeling that time was elastic and that I'd been in the dark for weeks or months, and if I could just go back and have another drink maybe the doors would be open when I tried the theater again.

But I'd already spent most of my cash. I had enough to catch the subway back to Penn. I already had my return train ticket carefully placed in my wallet.

I folded the screenplay pages, stuck them in my jacket pocket, and walked.

Sometimes I looked for Kathy without even realizing I was doing it. I walked along the streets of Manhattan, gauging women's faces, noting expressions, hair color, jaw lines, hints of smiles, voices, sizes, thinking without fully grasping that I was even searching for her, but still somehow knowing that was exactly what I was doing.

Comprehension dawned when I found myself down at the South Street Seaport, staring out over the water, still thinking about her, imagining her down there in the east river. Then the full understanding of my day really began to dawn. I hadn't seen anyone except her, versions of her, women who didn't look anything like her, or what she would look like now if she'd lived to adulthood, but they were still all her.

The waves lapped over floating waste and flotsam that was not her corpse. Kathy had been so prevalent in my mind the whole day, like so many other days before, that I couldn't even add up the hours that had been forfeited to her. I wondered if she noted this wherever she was. If my small sacrifices sat stacked beside her, thigh-high, in paradise, purgatory, or hell.

My memories and dreams carried me on. It was a state of mind I was supposed to avoid according to all the doctors. I was always told to stay conscious of my surroundings, my own sense of self, time, and place. My psychiatrists used phrases like "retrain your brain." As if that was ever possible, as if it could ever happen. Who can stop doing the things that he does? Who can stop being who he is? It was like telling me not to like horror films anymore. It was like telling me to not carefully place my return train ticket in my wallet. It was like telling me not to notice my own failings. It was like telling me to forget my father's death.

Kathy Lark on the water, in the waves, drifting from one whitecap to the next, like a seagull moving in the mist. Retrain my brain. Refrain from pain. Rename the dame. Maybe if she'd gone missing as Madge she wouldn't matter as much to me. Blanche. Belinda. Claire. Edna. I thought of all the names I hated. My own was among them. How much easier it would be not to care then.

A homeless man watched me dawdling. He gave me a look that proved we were on the same wavelength, that he too was looking into the water for his lost love, his past, his home, his hope, his future among the flotsam. He pushed a shopping cart missing one wheel. It creaked and moaned, and I knew that among his empty cans and winter rags there would be wicker baskets he had woven to prove his sanity.

I'd run into a lot of guys like him on the ward. Once-proud professors or construction foremen or vice squad cops brought down by their own failed attempts to come to terms with their love or fears or anguish.

An ashtray he'd sculpted from a lump of clay. I knew it had begun as something else in his hands. He'd taken his clay and had pressed his thumbs into it adeptly, slowly massaging it the way he would caress his wife, his mistress, his dream woman. The clay would take the shape of his hopes and fantasies. A small, beautiful statue would appear of a waif with butterfly wings, the face of innocence, lips parted in a laugh the rest of us could hear. The orderlies would stalk past and say, "Hey, come on now, does that look like an ashtray to you? If you want, you could make a pot holder too," and with their huge, unforgiving fists they'd pound our aspirations and faith back into a smashed mass of clay.

Then we'd make our ashtrays, potholders, and handcrafted baskets, and the orderlies would sell them at the SoHo street fair every Saturday and pick up a couple hundred extra bucks to keep the cash flow for their meth deals sanguine.

Sometimes the orderlies would stage cage matches between the wards. Ward C and Ward D had the toughest combatants. We'd wear our garbage can lids over our chests and our helmets made from metal colanders and do battle with hammers and hedge clippers. The orderlies didn't mind if we fought to the death.

Depending on how the depressives, homicidal maniacs, and suicides were holding up, it could actually be considered a kind of therapy. The rage being let loose, the melancholia and boredom being staved off. The paperwork could be faked so it appeared the dead had been released weeks earlier. Then the first-year med students from the local hospital would be called. They'd come by and remove organs, pack them in dry ice and sell them on the black market.

The homeless guy locked eyes with me. He touched his belly. I knew the code. He was telling me they'd taken one of his kidneys and his spleen. I crossed my arm over my chest and thumped my heart with my fist, like a Roman soldier hailing his brother.

I wanted to walk up and ask him WHY IS THE GIRL IN THE BOX AND NOT IN THE BOWL? I wondered if he, too, agreed that I SHOULD CLARIFY THE ROLE OF THE MEMENTO THIEF. Maybe he could explain to me IS IT A'S FATHER OR B'S BROTHER? We could sit and discuss exactly WHEN DID HIS LEG GET CUT OFF AND IS IT THE SAME LEG IN THE BATHTUB? If we threw down a few shots of Jameson's I could almost guarantee that he would tell me WHO LEFT THE OLD LADY'S CORPSE ON THE ROOF? Did he, too, REALLY LIKE THE OLD MAN WITH ONLY HALF A FACE AND THE SHOTGUN? Would he demand that I BRING HIM BACK IN FOR THE THIRD ACT? Would he want to know if HIS DAUGHTER HAS BIG TITS? Did it keep him up late at night, while he was pushing his cart, his curiosity blazing while he beseeched WHO KILLED THE MOUSE? I could see him picking up a half-smoked butt off the sidewalk and pressing it between his teeth as he leaned in and inquired IS THE MEMENTO THIEF IN THE HOUSE? Perhaps he knew all the

Tom Piccirilli

names of all the characters and could sit and draw me graphs and maps as he elaborated on whether A'S FATHER HELPED HIM ESCAPE FROM THE SICK NEIGHBOR. And we could re-enact through dialogue all our inner conflict as we drew weapons from the shed and dramatized all that GREAT TENSION BETWEEN THE KID AND THE GUY WITH THE SHOVEL. Maybe he could tell me who I was supposed to be. Maybe I was the kid. Maybe I was the guy. Maybe I was the shovel.

The homeless man walked over like he had all the answers I was seeking. Different possibilities ran through my mind. He was one of the psychiatrists from the hospital sent to keep an eye on me while he witnessed the effects of some radical new treatment involving hypnosis and nanobytes. He was a dethroned king who needed my help to unseat his evil twin brother, Maynard, who had stolen his rightful place as leader of the small country Hysteria. He was a future version of me come back to tell me how to avoid winding up on the streets like him.

"Spare a couple bucks?" he asked.

"Sorry."

"God bless you."

"You too."

I checked his eyes. They were a pale blue, thick with cataracts. Mine were brown. Maybe this was what happened in the future due to sunspots and intense radiation. He held his grubby hand out and I took it.

I turned and walked on. The liquor continued to make its way through me, easing into my muscles, cooling the flame of my mind.

I touched my belly again. I suddenly remembered why I had tried to hara-kiri myself. It wasn't just to die. It was so I could cut out the Komodo dragon ghost that was living inside me.

The Komodo dragon's name was Gideon. Gideon had been with me since I was a kid. He had shown up one day when I was still in the crib, crawled inside me, and that was that.

Gideon had things on his mind. Sometimes he was inside my guts, sometimes he ran loose and left me terse Post-its

42

written in an angry block print not all that different from Monty's handwriting.

Gideon wasn't from Komodo at all but from the nearby Indonesian island of Gili Dasami. A member of the monitor lizard family, *Varanidae*, he belonged to the largest living species of lizard, having grown to 9.9 feet and weighing almost two hundred pounds before he was killed by an early hominid during the Pleistocene Age. His fossil was currently on display at the Queensland Museum in Australia.

Evolutionary development of the Komodo started with the *Varanus* genus, which originated in Asia about 38 million years ago and migrated to Australia. Around 15 million years ago, a collision between Australian and Southeast Asian land masses allowed the varanids to move into what is now called the Indonesian archipelago. A lowering of sea level during the last glacial period divulged extensive stretches of continental shelf that the Komodo colonized, and they soon became isolated in their present island range as sea levels rose in the millennia that followed.

I've never cracked a book on the subject. Gideon had made a study of his own species, and occasionally shared information, leaving me maps and documentation.

Gideon's tail was as long as his body. He had sixty serrated teeth, which were often lost and replaced. His saliva was usually blood-tinged because his teeth were almost completely covered by gingival tissue that was naturally lacerated during feeding. He had a long, yellow, deeply forked tongue. He had poor night vision. He had a habit of swinging his head from side to side as he walked. He ate mostly deer and carrion. Some of his scales were reinforced with bone and had sensory plaques connected to nerves that facilitated his sense of touch.

He was capable of sprinting up to about fifteen miles per hour for brief periods. When I was little, Gideon used to chase me around the back yard. I would scream and my ma would wave to me from the kitchen window.

He climbed trees on our property proficiently using his

powerful claws. To catch prey that's out of reach, the Komodo dragon may stand on its hind legs and use its tail as a support. Gideon used to do that a lot after chasing my cousin Jane up into the maples, but she doesn't remember.

The Komodo dragon was a vulnerable species and was found on the IUCN Red List. There were approximately four to five thousand Komodo dragons remaining in the wild, restricted to the islands of Gili Motang, Gili Dasami, Rinca, Komodo, and Flores.

Komodo dragons avoided encounters with humans. Juveniles were very shy and would flee quickly into a hideout if a human came closer than about three hundred feet. Older animals would also retreat from humans from a shorter distance away. If cornered, they would react aggressively by gaping their mouths, hissing, and swinging their tails. If they were disturbed further, they might start to attack and bite. Only a very few cases were the result of unprovoked attacks by abnormal individual dragons that had lost their fear toward humans.

Gideon was one of those abnormal individuals, which was why his ghost lived inside me, moving about, waiting patiently. For what, I didn't know.

I knew I should go back to Monty's office and try to have a real conversation with him for once. Make him understand that I needed help. Ask him about his notations, figure out who'd sent the script, if it was me or some other crazier version of me, someone drunker, someone smarter, someone who knew what he wanted in the world and understood how to get it. If it was any of them, I'd gladly step aside.

Maybe Monty could talk me out of the writing business. Maybe he could hook me up with Bango and I could team up with other angry clowns and smack the shit out of rich fascist pricks who wouldn't allow me health care. I had big flat feet to begin with. I looked forward to wearing oversized clown shoes for a cause and producing verifiable results. Offer more tax breaks or I'll bust your ass with these size seventeens. Suck my fat toes, wealthy scum!

I wanted another drink. I checked my wallet for a folded-up twenty or fifty. My mother used to do that to me when I was a teen. Emergency cash. She'd fold it into a little nub of a square and then not tell me it was in there. First time I found it was when I was handing a state trooper my license and he thought I was bribing him. The statie asked, "Are you offering me remittance to let you go without a ticket?" I didn't know what to say. I stared straight ahead through the windshield, dreaming about standing on the pedal and having a three-state high speed chase with millions in damage.

The trooper took the money and gave me a ticket anyway. I appreciated that. It taught me a lesson about the value of money and the law.

I passed the usual places in SoHo, Little Italy, Chinatown, moved up through the streets like a sea creature moving up through the depths into the shallows. The bookstores and movie shops called to me like my dreams begging for another chance to guide me to them. I looked up into the sky and tried to call down rain. It was a day when I should have been walking in the rain, with the wind rising around me, the dark funnel clouds opening above me, a mean storm waiting to break. So below, as above.

But there wasn't any rain. The world denied me my tempest. The alcohol gave me a sour stomach. Gideon curled and uncurled upon a sharp flat rock inside me. The scent of citrus and garlic came on heavy. The smell of freshly made tomato sauce made my belly growl. Gideon hissed in response. Maybe I could get Monty to spring for a slice of pizza. I kept fighting my way back toward his office. I had his notes in my head trying to fight their way back out again. I wanted to know about the powerful roles that actors on their way up or on their way down would hope to play.

Maybe Glory Greer could read my script out to me. Maybe I'd do better dictating it to her rather than trying to write it.

Maybe I had to get crazy wasted again and just hope that the other me could finish the fucking thing and email the rest of it off to Monty by Monday. That other version, he had to know how much was riding on this already. Otherwise, why would it be good enough to have garnered Monty's interest once again?

The foot traffic swelled and swarmed and eased again. I liked city noise. The music, the voices, the car horns, ambulances, all the immense tourist babble. It served to cover over my own thoughts. For whole blocks I didn't have to hear myself think.

When I finally made it back to Monty's building and up the five floors I found his door locked. He'd left for the day, maybe to take a meeting with a client or business associate. More likely he was perched at a bar waiting for the twenty-something cutie-pies to show up so he could hand out his cards and ask them if they'd ever thought about being in show business. There was a reason why pissed off women shackled him to beds in reindeer costumes with spider monkeys on the loose.

I ducked into the Vietnamese restaurant just to make sure he wasn't hiding out in there, waiting for the delivery girl to get back so he could bird-dog her some more.

I had nothing to do and nowhere to go. I was drinking again and should check myself back into a clinic someplace. I had a screenplay to finish, one that my apathetic agent was actually showing some excitement over. I had to get my head on straight enough to at least read the damn thing. I had to get in touch with my other self and get him to knock out the other two acts. I had to get out of my mother's basement. I needed to find Kathy's killer. I had a lot to do and every direction to run.

So I sat there as the waiter smiled brightly and asked in pidgin and through body language if I wanted sweet beer and dinner. I grinned back at him and waved him off and slipped out the door back onto the street. I walked past Monty's building again. I thought of Zypho and wondered if the new script was in any way related to the alien from beyond the edge of space. I was curious about whether the answer to all of Monty's questions lay within reach of Zypho's tentacles.

WHAT MAKES YOU DIE

I stood in front of the Weird Sisters store. The place made me think of *Macbeth*. I remembered seeing the play for the first time on stage off-Broadway with my sophomore English class. The lead actor made the unfortunate choice of giving Macbeth a thick Scottish accent like Welles did in his film version. It taught me a lot about how dialogue could enrapture an audience or push them away. Not only the meaning and rhythm of the words, but the sound of them, the power of them.

I stepped into the shop and a faint stink assailed me. It was the unmistakable smell of rotting meat.

The store was packed with shelves stuffed with jars, bottles, and other containers filled with the likes of foxfire, salamander glands, dried mistletoe, salt, incense, goofer dust (graveyard), goofer dust (crematorium), dried doves' blood, owl liver, goat hooves, bats' wings, rooster hearts, and red peppers. I wondered if they threw it around or made stew with it.

There were ceremonial daggers, chalices, and candles of every color on display. I looked for eye of newt but didn't see any anywhere, and yet I wondered if they were someplace looking at me. I wondered if any of this was real. I thought if it was then animal activists would be down here protesting the place night and day.

Other shelves contained reference materials, maps of haunted towns, houses, and castles. I picked up a book called *Witches and Witchcraft* and paged through it. Leaning against a case full of different colored chalks that aided you in drawing pentagrams and circles of protection, I read about scrying mirrors, divination, the power of names, drawing down the moon, numerology, the sabbat, and how witches sometimes danced around a lightning-struck dead coven tree.

A young woman of maybe twenty-five, who looked more like the girl next door than anyone working in a shop that sold rooster hearts and goat hooves should, approached.

She said, "I'm sorry if I kept you waiting. I didn't hear you come in. I was in the back room. Can I help you?"

I wondered what happened in the back room. Maybe they kept some sheared-off dead limbs from a lightning-split tree back there. My head filled with the wrong pictures. I could feel them surge. I fought them down. I saw her dancing, naked, singing prayers, while her sisters stirred a bubbling vat of human fat. I knew at least five directors who would love a scene like that, who would pay me serious cash for it.

I put the book back and said, "I have no idea. It depends, I suppose. Are you a good witch or a bad witch?"

It made her smile. It was a pretty smile that reached her eyes. You didn't see that much in L.A. "You've never been in a store like ours before."

"No."

"How did you find us?"

"My agent's office is next door."

"Oh, him. He's an asshole."

I let out a chuckle. "And you probably didn't even have to use any heightened sense of perception to pick up on that."

I thought of New York real estate. I imagined just how much of this stuff the owner had to push every day just to make the rent. How many hundreds or even thousands of urbanites were sitting around right now drawing circles of protection around themselves in fifth floor walk-ups.

"My name's Eva," she said.

"Names have power."

"Yes, they do."

"Yours isn't particularly witchy."

"Well... Eve was the first woman, born with a thirst for knowledge. Therefore, the first witch. That's all that white magic is. The will and desire to learn about those things not generally addressed or admitted."

I couldn't seem to stop talking. I didn't know where this chattiness was coming from. The sound of my own voice was difficult to recognize. "Some people might say that Eve's desire is what doomed the humanity to a loss of grace."

"Some people are dull-witted, sexist, puritanical fanatics who prefer to live in willful ignorance."

"Many, in fact."

"But not you."

"No, I don't think so."

"What can I help you with?"

She had green eyes flecked with gold, blonde hair fixed into a bouncing ponytail. She was a cheerleader type. I could imagine her on the sidelines doing kicks and clapping as the quarterback sprinted toward the end field. But her clothing wrecked the girl-next-door image. She wore a wrap covered with the Weird Sisters logo, three witches with their backs to a boiling cauldron. One a crone, one a kind of buxomly mother figure, and the last a seductive teen. On her blouse were ancient symbols, inscriptions in Latin, and verses from the Bible. Her leggings were black with bright white star constellations and signs of the zodiac.

"What about stealing a soul?"

"Excuse me?"

"Where can someone learn how to poach a man's shadow, his spirit, and stick it in a jar and watch it writhe in torment?"

Eva set her lips and her expression shifted to sadness, interest, and futility. "I can't help you with anything like that. The things we sell are mostly for wiccan rites, pagan beliefs that are in keeping with the harmony of the earth."

"Good," I said. "I'm glad. I was afraid you were going to tell me it happens all the time."

She glanced around, but we were still alone in the store. I couldn't be the strangest cat who ever came into the store, could I? I wondered if she was going to split out the back, call a cop. Maybe hurl goofer dust (crematorium) into my eyes.

She stepped in closer to me, her gaze growing more serious. The dimples faded. Her chin came up.

"Something's happened to you," she said. "You're in real pain." She looked deep into my face and saw something there that put fear into her.

"Something's happened to everybody," I said.

"No, not like you."

"I got a chance to carry the ball for a while, and then I dropped it, that's all." I gestured to the front window and the city beyond it. "Damn near everybody shares the same story."

"You're thick with ghosts."

My breath caught in my chest. Maybe it was the hard sell. Maybe I was an easy mark. Somebody who visits a psychic is clearly in need of some kind of reassurance. Ten thousand fake spiritualists down through the ages have exploited their victims' obvious weaknesses.

"You have to understand that there's a balance," she explained. "Where there's grace, there's depravity. Where there's salvation, there's Satan. Confusion leads to clarity. The deeper your bewilderment, the greater your spiritual comprehension in the end."

"And will red peppers and salamander glands help me out on that?"

Eva squared her shoulders. "Now you're belittling the very thing you asked about."

"I tend to do that," I said.

"The gods always know your heart. And so does the devil."

Now, that felt very true to me.

She rubbed the back of her hand against her nose. It was a cute nose. She sort of smiled again, trying to remain amiable despite the heaviness I'd laid on her in our discussion. I wondered what had diverted her into working in a shop like this when she should be at some booth on Coney Island letting the boys ogle and flirt with her and buy her cotton candy. I had romanticized notions of the world where pretty girls like this were concerned.

She said, "Maybe I can help."

"I can pay you."

"Don't taint my efforts. Let my willingness be pure."

"Okay."

She turned and moved up the aisle, her ponytail swaying,

turned the corner and vanished. I thought of taking her home with me and introducing her to the family. This is my ma. This is my sister. This is the Jack of Spades. This is Lawrence Welk. This is the baby in the bin.

I waited. I tried not to think about her in the back room covered in witches' oil. I took another book off the shelf and continued reading, learning about how pagan rites could be either white: right-handed, clockwise, righteous, and graceful — or black: left-handed, widdershins or counter-clockwise, flying in the face of the natural order of the world. I wondered how much foxfire and dozens of pounds of owls' livers it would take for me to regain whatever it was that I'd lost.

Eva returned. There was a smudge of chalk on her forearm, like she'd been spelling my name in a pentagram alongside those of angels and demons, except I hadn't told her it yet. Michael, Raphael, Azazeal, Beli ya'al, Leviathan. My name of power would stay with me alone for a little while longer. She smiled sadly at me. She put a hand to the side of my face and said, "I see that a dragon lives inside you."

Around the corner was a small coffee shop where they served fresh baked goods. I went through my wallet again and, sure enough, I found a fifty dollar bill folded countless times until it was practically the size of a postage stamp. Emergency cash my mother had never told me about. My ma. Did you drive me over the big ledge or did I drive you?

I ate two salt bagels with butter. The docs had told me not only to quit drinking but to watch what I ate. I had a tendency toward high blood pressure, low blood sugar, migraines, palpitations, angina, and my cholesterol was for shit.

But I had impulse control issues. At the moment I was trying hard not to sneak a kiss from Eva, who sat across from me sipping an espresso and daintily eating a biscotti while our eyes occasionally met and she favored me with a sweet grin.

She'd taken off her wrap. Beneath it she wore a black sleeveless T-shirt with the word PRESENCE on it. I didn't understand the reference. Was she stating that she had presence, which I agreed with, or was she declaring that everyone else should do more to evoke a sense of attendance and dignity? Around her right bicep she was adorned with a thin armband tattoo.

Finally, I said, "My name is Tommy Pic. It's not a secret, but I'm starting to feel as if I'm willfully keeping it from you so that you or someone else doesn't lay a curse on me."

"I promise I won't," she said. "Promises have power too."

"Tell me how you know so much about me."

"Some people can see such things. I'm one of them."

"So it's not a witchy skill you earned from sacrificing chickens in the dark?"

"You're being glib again."

"I told you I tended to do that."

"Yes, you did. I failed to mention that I don't like it much."

"I'll make a conscious effort to refrain."

She cocked her chin at me even as she took another bite of the biscotti. I liked the gesture. I liked her teeth. I liked her chin. Crumbs clung to her lips. My impulse control issues mounted. I very much wanted to kiss her. She with sweetness on her lips and me with salt. Sometimes we have to search for our symbols, sometimes they find us waiting.

I asked her to tell me her story and she did.

She was twenty-six, born in an Ohio burg called Stow, daughter of a disgraced brimstone preacher whose congregation had forsaken him after he got caught with an underage male prostitute and enough methamphetamines to kill a bull elephant. She was a graduate of NYU with a business degree, trained in something corporate I didn't understand and that she never wanted to be a part of anyway. Her roommate was a late-blooming punk rock Goth-wannabe years after the Goth movement had already turned puerile and punk rock was a nearly forgotten part of rock 'n' roll history.

But if New York did anything, it offered numbers. Whatever your interest, your hobby, your cause, or your curiosity, whether cutting edge, fashion-forward, retro, vintage, illegal, or esoteric, you could find someone someplace on the same wavelength. Eva had started hitting the underground club scene and running into more and more people who claimed to be wiccan and wore pentacles, called on goddesses of the hunt, and said shit like, "Do what thou wilt." She was still angry with her father and pissed off at God, and lost in a world of self-doubt with no clear path.

A friend worked part time at Weird Sisters and Eva started taking shifts and reading the books in stock and playing with the ceremonial stuff and performing small rites of thanks and positive reinforcement. She believed in the root basics of witchcraft, that people could exert influence on the natural order through concentration, sacrifice, prayer, and ritual. Somewhere along the way she acquired, she said, a kind of sensitivity to energies and forces some people might describe as supernatural or occult.

She laid it all out without any kind of embarrassment or excuses at all. I got a feeling that she trusted me for reasons I didn't wholly understand. I bought her another espresso and biscotti and stared at her chest. I liked the thrust of her moderate breasts. I liked the word PRESENCE and sought to unlock its meaning.

I studied her tattoo. I liked unobtrusive tattoos on women. It seemed to be script bordered by two bands. I tried to make out what it said. It made me think that language mattered a great deal to Eva.

She didn't say anything at all about men. I'd already scoped her fingers for rings. She wore a lot of them, some mere bands of silver, several a lot more ornate, but nothing on the ring finger of her left hand. I felt a flush of elation that I tried to tamp down.

She eyed me carefully. Her gaze flitted about me on occasion like she was watching wisps of smoke drifting from my clothes. It got me a little paranoid. I was already a little paranoid, so the feeling was nothing new. And I liked her watching me.

"And now you?" she asked.

I didn't know where to start. What to leave in, what to censor, how many lies to tell. I began with Zypho. Zypho was always a good place to begin. Almost everybody had seen a couple of the movies in the series, even if they thought they were awful, which they were. Nobody knew my better films. I could barely remember the titles myself. They'd been so long ago. Waves of self-pity began surging and breaking against my inner landscape. Eva spotted it happening and reached across the table and put her fingers lightly to my wrist.

"Now you, Tommy," she said.

I didn't start with Zypho. I started with my father and the movies. I ran it out in as straight a line as I could. It wasn't too bad until I got to the constant flops in L.A., the mounting failures. Then I began to lose my time frame. I kept stopping myself trying to get things in their correct order. But they didn't have an order, they all hit at once. When I mentioned Tony, Kathy, and Gideon, she nodded and her hand became more insistent upon my wrist. It was a pleasant feeling. But something somewhere was distracting me. I felt nauseous. Maybe the dragon was laying eggs inside of me. I started to sweat. I scanned the room. I knew what the problem was.

It was the sound of all the folks tapping away on the keyboards of their laptops. The writers proving they were writers because they were writing in a coffee shop with other writers writing in a coffee shop. They were all knocking out their poetry, telling their life stories, finishing columns for their blogs and websites, working on their great American novels. Some of them were composing scripts. Some of them might even have been repped by Monty. I looked in their faces and was again searching for Kathy Lark. Maybe she was among us. Maybe she would finally come out of hiding. Maybe her memoir about vanishing for nearly thirty years would top the bestseller lists. The sound of typing was deafening.

"What is it, Tommy?"

"Don't call me that," I said.

"But—"

"My name is Tom. You know how condescending it is for a grown man to be called Tommy? Jesus, fuck!"

"You told me to call you that."

"What am I, six years old?"

Eva didn't shush me, she shhhhed me. A soft, gentle sound as she leaned in closer, as her fingers moved up my forearm even farther. Gideon reared and hissed. Eva shhhed him too. She got a clean napkin and dabbed at my forehead, my upper lip. I hoped to Christ I wasn't crying. I glanced around and nobody had noticed shit. Yeah, keep writing, kids, that's the way to show the world you're observant, that you notice the details of your neighbors, your brothers and sisters.

Perhaps they knew why the girl was in the box and not in the bowl. Who left the old lady's corpse on the roof? They couldn't wait to get to the next stanza so they could describe in iambic pentameter the old man with the shotgun and half a face. For all I knew they could be emailing each other from three feet away, discussing the memento thief in the house. I felt like flinging Monty's notes in the air and watching them all dive for the pages. Anything so they'd just stop clacking their keyboards for ten seconds of cool silence.

I stood and said, "How can you help me?"

She said, "Let's go for a walk. Tom."

I couldn't remember the last time I had walked arm in arm with a pretty girl. Maybe while I was still married to my ex-wife, except I didn't remember walking with her much. We tended to chase each other around a lot. Either with a burning need or full of rage. We either landed in bed or hit the floor fighting or fucking. She could make my skin overheat like white-hot wire. She had a wicked left hook. She dreaded my nightmares. I sometimes awoke to find her huddled on a chair, watching me. She said I talked a lot in my sleep, and the voice I spoke with was hardly ever my own.

Tom Piccirilli

I found that I was telling this all to Eva. She listened with interest and without apparent judgment. I was waiting for her to bolt. She didn't. I watched her eyes and I tried to read her tattoo again. I failed. My eyes were for shit. I should've just asked her, but the mystery somehow excited me. I pictured that they were lines from the great classical poems of the world. Baudelaire, Poe, Eliot, Sexton, Plath, Berryman, Rimbaud, Keats. I let my imagination run wild and saw my dialogue wrapped around her flesh. Zypho, you beast of a thousand broken hearts, leave the people of our world now and return to the black void of your evil galaxy. Zypho, get your tentacles out of my wife's vagina.

We walked down to Union Square and sat beside each other on a stone bench surrounding a fountain that wasn't on. I always wondered what attending NYU would've done for my career. A little more time to be a kid here in the city before I'd rushed out to the West Coast. More time to mature on eastern turf, enjoying the seasons before being pitched out into the blazing, unchanging sunlight of California. Maybe it would've mattered; maybe it just would've made things worse. The shrinks always warned me against spending too much time dwelling on regrets and thinking about the paths I could've taken, rather than dealing with the ones I had taken and trying to find a way back to the good times. I just wasn't sure what the good times were, when they'd been, how I'd handled them.

I waited for Eva to explain how she could help me. I thought she planned on brewing some concoction with black cat whiskers, the ears of a hanged man, fingernails clipped from a stillborn baby, all kinds of heinous shit, and then I'd have to drink it in a graveyard at midnight beneath a full moon and some kind of cosmic curse would be lifted. But I glanced at her grin and the bobbing ponytail, the amused hazel eyes, and I realized we weren't going to get that funky at all no matter how many magic books she was surrounded by. We were still arm in arm on the bench and she said, "I'm having a party Friday night. I think you should come."

"Is this a party with onion dip and cocktails, or is this a coven gathering where you and twelve other members of a coven stand around a tree and point athames toward the sky and invoke spirits to possess you?"

"The onion dip kind." She smiled, and I couldn't help but return it. "But some of my friends are also white witches. And they might be able to guide you."

"Guide me where?"

"To wherever you need to go to find some peace."

"Oh."

We walked around Washington Square. We did a little window shopping. She told little aimless stories about her friends, customers at the Weird Sisters, her boss who didn't believe in witchcraft but had seen an opportunity to make some bank after reading a *Wall Street Journal* article about the rise of Wicca in recent years. Most desperate people turned to a belief in a higher power when things got bad enough. They stopped in for love spells, to have their fortunes told, to perform sacred rites that might protect them in dark times, that might save their loved ones. The worse things got, the more people wanted to hold some kind of power in their hands. Most churches didn't even let you light candles anymore. You had to pay ten bucks just to switch a switch and watch light bulb flicker on a fake votive.

I believed her. I could fully understand folks' reasoning. Who knew, if I hadn't tumbled to her shop by accident I might've one day sought it out anyway. How much stranger was it to put your faith in ancient magic as opposed to the power of making ashtrays?

We stopped in a used bookstore. I watched her wander up the aisle, skirting huge stacks of novels on either side. I followed and toppled books left and right. The owner of the place was used to it and didn't even look up from his pillbox station at the front of the shop. He looked like a Japanese soldier dug in on Guadalcanal. Eva's ponytail bobbed and flicked left and right. Every time it gave me a clear view of the back of her neck I felt my chest tighten. She plucked books from various sections. Science fiction, crime, the clas-sics. Biographies and autobiographies on filmmakers. Some of them were famous. Some nobody but cats like me had ever heard of. I continued following her. I didn't strike off on my own although I loved, or used to love, spending hours in stores exactly like this one.

She came to the plays and poetry section. She clutched a handful. Then she found screenplays. She found two or three and tossed them on top. She carried twenty pounds of books. Her muscles flexed. Her biceps stood out like a ten-nis ball. She finally pressed the books into my arms and said, "Here."

I carried them up to the front of the store and waited like the world's most patient boyfriend while she paid over thirty bucks. The owner snapped open a shopping bag and carefully placed the used books inside. Once we hit the street, she hand-ed me the bag and said, "My gift to you."

"Eva—"

"Don't say you can't take them. They're my gift."

"I'm a writer. I'm a big reader, or used to be. How do you know I don't already own most of these?"

"It doesn't matter. These are my gift. These copies will be different. Haven't you ever received the same gift from two people, and somehow they still felt different to you? You liked one over the over for some reason?"

"I don't know," I said. "I don't think so."

"Of course you have. It's not always the gift that matters, you know. It's the spirit in which it is given. The offering itself has virtue and influence."

"Do you make these offerings to all the jagoff losers who happen to wander into your shop?"

"I help people I like, if I can."

I held the bag and felt the weight of half a million words. Included in that weight was the kindness and im-plied influence of Eva's gift. I wondered if she thought this would get me back on track. If these words would help me to find my own again. If I could exorcize Zypho this way. If I could charm my ghosts.

"I've got to get back to work."

I walked her back to the Weird Sisters. The Vietnamese delivery girl almost ran us down on the sidewalk as she raced past. I had forty minutes to make the next train out of Penn. I let my imagination run a little wild about what could be done in forty minutes. I pictured Eva and I making love in the back room of the shop amid the remainders of scuffed stars of Solomon drawn in chalk, keys of angelic names, blobs of melted candle wax, and chicken feathers. Forty minutes was enough time to profess eternal love, to dance the Tarantella, to read her most of *A Season in Hell* and *Flowers of Evil*. We could get to the part in *Zypho: Critter from Beyond the Edge of Space* where Zypho sucks out the brainpan fluid of the lady CIA agent holding him captive in Area 52. In the Japanese kiddie version we could get up to the part where Zypho is being nunchucked almost to death by a magical preteen girl in a yellow spacesuit with pigtails flailing. In the XXX version, Zypho would be in the middle of an orgy getting his tentacles sucked by men and women alike. The scene would feature the return of 70s porn star Selena Flower. Selena Flower was pushing sixty-five and still damn flexible, and proved it over and over during the orgy, including the twenty-man pileup at the end.

"Thank you for the gifts," I said.

"My pleasure. And I'll see you Friday, yes?"

"Sure." The Monday after, Monty and I were headed back to L.A. Maybe some magic would wear off on me and I'd be able to get at least a second act finished. "Who else is going to be at your party?"

"Friends, of course." She slipped a hand into my jacket and pulled my phone free. She put her home and work phone into it. "You can bring someone if you like."

"My agent?"

"No. No, please, not that asshole."

I wondered if Bango would like to show up. I thought Bango and I could share a lot of similar stories and really understand one another as comrades in arms.

She opened the door to the shop and took a step in. My heart dodged left. My breath hitched. My blood buzzed. I didn't want to let her go. There was always a living terror inside me that thought, This is it, if I let her go now I'll never see her again. She will vanish. She will cease to exist. You'll return to tomorrow only to discover that she never was. No one will remember seeing her with you. They'll say you were alone.

"Give me a call this week and I'll give you my address," Eva said.

"Okay."

She withdrew, turned, moved to me again, and pecked my cheek. It was chaste. It was innocent. It was sexier than anything I'd ever seen Selena Flowers ever do with man, woman, or critter from beyond the edge of space. The door to the store closed and I backed away and walked to the corner. I stood there for a while thinking that, finally, after all this time back in New York, I at last felt like I had some real presence.

I caught the C train, made it to Penn, and stood around with a couple hundred other people staring up at the tote board to see which track our train would be leaving on. I didn't care that much. I sat in the waiting room and waited for them all to bolt. Regular daily commuters like to get the same seats. Seats up front that would land them directly at the staircases where they'd parked their cars at their particular stations. It was important to them to save a minute or two wherever they could. They spent their lives working jobs they hated, for bosses they despised, for money that was already long spent. You were never quite so aware that you were growing old as when you were waiting for a train that refused to arrive.

The track number came up and the mob moved like the undead following the pulse of the living. I clambered to my feet and flowed along. We shuffled and shambled down the stairs and shouldered our way into the rail cars.

I slid into a window seat with my bag of books and thought about Eva, who knew me better than anyone else alive and who barely knew me at all. I saw the cookie crumbs on her lips again. I'd missed my chance. I'd wussed out. I should've made a move. It was the perfect time. The symbol had force. I knew it would haunt me until I kissed her, and it would haunt me for fifty years afterward. I would write about it forever. The salt on my lips, the sweet on hers. It would show up in every movie I ever did from this day on.

I opened the script again to *What Makes You Die*. I liked the title. I wanted to give a nod to my other self and say, Good job, there, Sparky. I felt wild inside but I thought I could make out the words this time. The train started to pull out of the station. We swam down a dark tunnel and the lights flickered and we rushed beneath the city and the East River and every second brought me closer to my ma's basement. I started to tremble. The lights flickered back on. We slid up to ground level again and I looked at the dirty buildings and cruddy yards of the buildings that backed up to the train tracks. Trash and paper and graffiti covered everything.

I tried to focus on the pages. Twenty-weight laser paper, the kind I used. My name right there on the title page. I looked at the tips of my fingers and thought, Well, boys, is any of it coming back yet? My fingers were stoically reticent.

My eyes were even worse. They refused to settle on the page. It was hysterical blindness. A wall of fear kept me from the writing. I knew that whatever was down there would hurt. I couldn't take any more hurt right now. I thought of seeing something about my father on those pages. Tony, my sister, my ex, the children I didn't have, the Pacific Ocean I had never once swam in during all the years I was in L.A., boxed up in my office more aware of my dreams than my life. I wonder if the ghost chasers were in there running around my house. I wonder if bitter priests moved through scenes.

Whose leg was in the goddamn bathtub? Was it A's father or B's brother? I desperately wanted to clarify the role of the memento thief. I wanted to know what the fuck a memento thief was and why I felt it was necessary to stick him in this screenplay. Maybe I could ask my cousin Jane to read the entire thing to me. But could I trust a woman who might've brought a baby to the bin? I said the name "Kathy" aloud. Kathy would help me, I thought. I knew it with more certainty than I knew anything. I didn't know if she was alive but I knew she would do everything she could to help me.

I pressed my head to the train's cold window. The rumbling vibrations went through me and jounced my skull off the glass, rap rap rap, like someone was knocking to be let in or let out. I wondered how much liquor it was going to take to bring my other self forward again. How much blood I might have to lose this time. If I'd have to wind up back on the ward battling the schizes and the sociopaths with shanks made from snapped toothbrushes and tuna can tops.

"Tickets, please."

My presence was fading. The passengers worked on their laptops on the way home, too. I didn't know where all this mad drive came from. They'd just put in a full day of work on Wall Street, importing-exporting, building towers, hiding nuclear waste, so why did they have to keep working now on the way home to Long Island?

What great literature could they be composing with no other inspiration than the dirty tracks to either side of the train windows or the empty faces of their fellow passengers? I glanced around and occasionally someone would look up and find something in my expression and then suddenly pound out another paragraph.

"Tickets, please."

Those were my sentences, I wanted to tell them. That's my metaphor, that's a description that was given to me by God. You've no right to it. You've no claim on it. Go hide on your own ward and wait for the doctors to try primal therapy with you. Scream until your throat is scorched and see how well it does for you. Cover your kidneys. Cut free your own phantoms.

"Tickets, please."

The conductor arose at my side like the angel of death expecting blood payment. He had his hand out and a smile of humble expectation. I thought, Here it is. I give him my ticket and finally the hell-bound train takes me away. My heart rate tripped along wildly. I checked my pockets for my ticket and wondered if I could pay for my passage with two silver coins instead. I didn't even have fifty cents, but it still made me wonder. The typing around me continued. Their hands worked together to a well-rehearsed symphony preparing for their crescendo. I wondered how many people I'd driven crazy with my keyboard. My ex had certainly gone around the bend. My landlady, my mother, various long-term relationships and one-night stands who would call me back to bed while I fought for that last perfect sentence, and somehow never attained it.

"Are you all right, sir?" the conductor asked.

"Yes."

"You don't look well."

"I'm fine, thanks."

"Ticket, please."

I checked my pockets, came up empty, then checked them again. I pulled out my wallet, and there it was, waiting to be found, as if my mother had planted it there months or years ago, having prophesied this very moment. I handed him my ticket. He punched it and stuck it in the little metal slot on my seat and moved on to the next car. A burst of fresh air blew into my face and I felt calmer.

I laid my head back and let the train rock and lull me into a tranquil state where I thought of Eva and nothing else. I opened my eyes fifteen minutes later and I felt as if I'd had a two-hour power nap. I dug around in the bag of books and came up with Barthelme's *The Dead Father*, a weirdo literary fantasy that I'd read a half dozen times before. I'd never met anyone else who'd read it, but Eva had clutched it to her chest and said, "Oh, this is a favorite." It didn't seem possible, but she was a witch.

I opened *The Dead Father* and found a Post-it note stuck to the inside of the front cover.

Gideon, my dragon, had written on it: DON'T GO TO HER PARTY ON FRIDAY. IT'S A TRICK. IT'S A TRAP. SHE WANTS TO COOK YOUR HEART AT MIDNIGHT.

The train pulled into my station. I got off, hit the steps, found my car in the lot, climbed in, and sat there smelling the faint scent of an oncoming storm. It brought the ocean inland and the clean aroma of frigid air from on high.

It wasn't really my car. It was my dead brother Bobby's car, an Impala with rusting quarter panels and a chipped windshield. He'd been eight years older than me. He'd died of hep C. Or maybe A or B. I didn't know the difference and didn't give a damn. He was an alcoholic bus driver who used to pull up in front of liquor stores while sixty or seventy passengers pulled the ding rope over and over. He'd died on our ma's couch, twice divorced with four kids who never saw him, not even when they'd heard he was about to croak. He had no money to bequeath them. He had no deathbed advice. He used to fuck lonely housewives on the floor at the back of the bus in between his morning and afternoon routes.

I didn't want to go home yet so I drove my usual pattern. I rolled out to Pilgrim State, swung around Suffolk Community College, and then on to the high school. I drew up to the front gate and thought about how the lunacy of ninth grade never ever leaves. Overwhelming delight, guilt, duty, the bitter embrace of adulthood. It set the tone for the rest of your life, and you judged everything based on what you knew at that time. Maybe I'd committed a crime by surviving this long, so much longer than Kathy Lark, if she was dead, and if she wasn't, maybe my crime was not having left with her.

There had to be more, I thought. There had to be greater traumas. There had to be deeper scars. Crimes must have been perpetuated against me. Did somebody tug on my tinkle in the boys' shower room? Did I partake in a gang rape against a retarded girl? One tiny torture is as good as another.

Sometimes I was fairly certain that I'd left my soul in the utility closet of seventh period study hall.

Busloads of kids were still leaving. Band, sports, cheerleading, half the student body seemed to never go home at all. They were always there in the halls, always around doing something or other. Their music was ghastly. I turned on my brother's radio. One of the buttons was still set to some oldies station he liked. He was eight years older than me; it sometimes felt like at least a full generation. We hadn't seen eye to eye on anything.

Boys skateboarded in the lot, grinding down the curbs and sidewalks. Sparks splashed and skittered. One bad oil leak under any of the cars and the whole lot would go up in an inferno. I halfway wanted to see it happen. A skater fell and tumbled with a stuntman's coordination, board scudding wildly and spinning on until it weakly bumped into a bus tire. I thought, We could've used that kid on the third Zypho sequel. The stunt crew on that one was third-rate at best. The guy in the monster suit was supposed to come down a chimney and kill a pair of lovers laid out in front of a romantic fire, and instead the tentacles had gone up and the stunt guy wound up in the hospital with minor burns on his arms and legs.

Girls were screaming, yelling about homework, makeup, places to meet up. The guys responded with their own love calls, shouts, crooning. It got my own pulse ticking harshly in my neck, all this action. I'd lived in lonely rooms for too long, watching movies without substance, reading books I couldn't remember.

Kids were smoking, necking, practicing the tuba. I hadn't thought things would change so much, but maybe it was just me who'd forgotten. A lot of them were probably thinking of

Hollywood right now. Being stars, living in Beverly Hills, walking the red carpets.

Whenever I missed the bus my mother would drop me off right out front, give me a kiss that got the tough kids rolling. I'd walk away in shame with the fuckers shoving at my back, playing kid games that skewered. And I'd turn to watch my mother's car drive off, abandoning me to the nexus of dismay and knowledge.

I punched the button for a new radio station but my dead brother Bobby had them all set to the same oldies one. Another old world crooner wearing a tuxedo, holding a Martini.

No strangers were allowed on school property, but I was no stranger. I'd spoken to English classes, drama classes, told the kids to never give up on their dreams. Everybody'd seen Zypho. I was famous. I eased up to the security booth. They actually had a black and white semaphore arm now that came down. More symbolism that just couldn't be overlooked. This was a tollbooth, and everyone had to pay just as heavy a price to get back in as they'd paid to get out in the first place.

The security guard was short and hairy, with the lines of a perpetual scowl seared into his features. It took me a few seconds to recognize him: Stevie Melton. A year or two older than me, he used to steal my lunch box and liked to smear my glasses with his plump, greasy thumbs. I heard he got one of his professors pregnant while he was failing at SCC. The kind of thing that should've been a disgrace but must've just made him feel proud when he had a beer with the boys. The professor left in the midst of a media blitz, had the kid, and moved back in with her parents. We all ran back to Ma. We all die on Ma's couch. Sometimes your life moved backward like you were on a conveyor belt.

Stevie Melton glowered. His sneer was twenty years older but no more refined than the last time I had seen it. A part of me wanted to bust through his little tollgate and smash his face into the Plexiglas window, but I knew he was thinking the same thing of me.

They'd given Stevie a badge that he'd kept polished like he was a real cop. He probably practiced ninja rolls in there, diving in and out of his little booth when no one was watching. I could tell by his eyes that he'd never seen his own kid and was terrified of the day when his child would come find him.

He knew me. He'd been waiting for me, and everyone like me, to return, and prove to him that I'd never become any better than him and everybody like him. The circle was never very large to begin with and it only became smaller. I wanted to ask him if he'd seen Kathy. I wanted to ask him if he'd murdered her. It was as possible as anything else.

I wondered if he could smell Eva's magic on me. I wondered if he had a dragon living inside him, too. I checked his little window to see if there were any Post-it notes on it. There were.

I had no plan, but suddenly a lie was on my lips. I had to get back my soul. "I'm here for the reunion committee."

It sounded weak even to me. Vague and facile.

"What reunion?" Stevie asked.

"'93."

"Who's the advisor?"

They had advisors for that sort of shit? Jesus. Talk about feeling sorry for someone. I was suddenly full of sympathy for those poor bastard teachers who spent decades here wasting their time at the front of the class and then actually had to stick around and advise guys like me twenty or thirty or forty years later and help get the reunions off the fucking ground. Goddamn.

I thought about the teacher least likely to ever participate in this sort of thing. He was ancient back then, but those are the ones who never die. They just petrified in their seats until they're hard as stone, and then they're used for bricks to build another hallway.

"Mr. Samuelson."

"Room 214."

"Thanks."

I drove in and parked, desperate for a drink. I should've stopped off at a liquor store first, picked up some whiskey to take the edge off. I shouldn't have come here at all, but where else could I go? Back home again to try to read a screenplay I couldn't remember, urging out another aspect of myself little by little, like holding a piece of cheese in front of a mouse hole? I got out of the car.

A sixteen-year-old girl, luscious, mystical, with a whirlwind of raven's hair swirling in the breeze, knocked me aside like the transparent, middle-aged creature I was. Gideon hissed. My ghosts asserted themselves; they held their ground, ready for a challenge.

A wash of impotent anger fired through me, and the tension made me feel strong and effective for two or three seconds. I was on her heels, the hair snapping into my face like a bullwhip. I almost welcomed its painful touch, hoping it would leave scars.

So I was returning to the scene of the crime. The mauled and mutilated lived in the walls. A fat kid with a kettle drum was banging along to Brahms' *Wiegenlied*. How fucking far was that going to get him in the outside world?

I stepped past the science labs, where you cut open worms, frogs, a piglet, a cow's eye, and, in my dreams, or maybe not, the starving Portuguese orphans who came on the black trucks that backed right up to the gym doors. Substitute teachers hustled them out while the lunch ladies squawked into megaphones, "*Nao toque nas paredes limpas. Nos estaremos alimentando-lhe muito peixe logo.*"

Don't touch the clean walls. We will be feeding you much fish shortly.

"*A festa de St. Peter comecara dentro da hora. Coloque mas tabelas e tenha uma sesta ate que esteja hora de comer.*"

The Feast of St. Peter will begin within the hour. Lie down on the tables and have a nap until it is time to eat.

I stood in front of my old locker, wondering if the combination would still work. If the pages I cut from newspapers and magazines about million-dollar scripts were still taped up inside.

"I don't think you're supposed to be here," someone behind me said.

You got that right. I turned and stared. She could've been any of the girls who'd refused to go out with me back then, when it mattered most. She smiled warmly and it sent an electrical thrill through me. No more than fifteen, she had a studious appearance—glasses, loose-hanging hair parted in the middle, a skirt and tie as if this were a private school, which it wasn't. She asked, "You lost?"

"Sorry. This your locker?"

"Yeah."

"Used to be mine about twenty years back. I was remembering a little."

"About a locker?"

"More or less."

"Okay," she acquiesced, still waiting. I wanted to ask her if the eviscerated Portuguese orphans crawled down the halls holding the flaps of their stomachs together with dirty hands, crying, *"Eu acredito que se encontraram me. Nao ha muitos peixes aqui."*

I believe they have lied to me. There is not much fish here.

Perhaps we'll meet again another two decades from now, both of us roaming about the school, staring at this same locker while some kid looks up into mad, sentimental faces.

"I'm gonna miss the bus."

"Oh. Excuse me," I said, flitting aside.

"Thanks a lot."

"What'd you stay late for?"

"Drama club."

"Oh."

"Yeah, you spoke to us once. I'm sorry, I don't remember your name. You made the Zypho movies, right?"

"Right."

"The first couple were pretty good."

I tried to grin, like I'd been let in on my own joke. I didn't think I was pulling it off.

"Were you going to give another talk to us?" she asked. "Everybody's gone now."

"No, not today. Maybe soon."

"That'd be cool."

She opened the locker and I saw that pages and pictures are still taped up inside the door, yellowed and grimy, but I don't know if they were the ones I put there. Newspaper clippings, magazine art, headlines. Twenty other kids had had this locker between me and her. I tried to read the articles but she grabbed a book and shut the door again. She took a breath and her ripening breasts thrust forward. I jumped back a step as if she'd snapped open a switchblade.

"Hey," she said, "this might sound funny, but—"

"I've got to get going."

"Yeah, well, I was just wondering if—"

I shrank away, wheeled about and damn near started scampering off. I'd never scampered before, I don't think, but I found it sort of fun. I'd never even said the word scamper before and now I couldn't stop. She followed for a few steps, trying to grab me by the elbow.

"Listen, some friends and I, we have a cinema appreciation club. It's at my house, in the garage, what used to be the garage, my dad fixed it up, turned it into a kind of TV room, except we already have a TV room. He wanted it to be his TV room, but my mother didn't like him always going in there, drinking beer, smoking cigars, so that was that. Now some friends and I watch Blu-rays, we hold like, little festivals, maybe you could come and speak to us? Doesn't have to be about Zypho. I loved your early films too. *Sleeping Where I Land, The Outlaw Light, The Way Down to Dream.* I've got them all on DVD. There's no commentaries. I'm something of a commentary freak. I like hearing the filmmakers talk about the movie, tell anecdotes, you know, all that. Maybe—" She faltered as I tried to stop scampering. "Maybe—"

"Sure," I said.

"When? Today?"

"Sure," I said. "I'd like that."

She pulled out a notebook and scrawled an address atop a piece of paper, then tore the sheet in half. "Here's where I live. No need to ring the doorbell. Just knock on the garage. We'll all be there by six. Is that a good time?"

"Sure," I said. "Perfect."

"I'm Celeste Campion, I head the group."

"I'm Tom—"

"I know who you are, Mr. Pic. Thanks again for this. It means a lot."

"My pleasure."

I turned a corner and a skinny boy arched like a vulture scooted out of the way. He was a hundred twenty pounds in white suede sneakers and dodged like I was part of the enemy lineup. His long hair flailed around his ears, little peach fuzz chin curling in flight. The fat kid with the kettle drum followed along, ka-bang ka-bang, playing in sync to the rhythm of my heartbeat.

I keep looking. What room was it? What was the number? The utilities closet of seventh period study hall. Three oh six? Three oh eight? I sort of lunged into 306 and saw shadows writhing in the corners. Two teachers screwing around, or two students making out, somebody giving head to the dead, or the smelly orphans still slinking around, trying to get their internal organs back.

Eu estarei escravendo ao congressista local immediamente. A remocao de meus intestines e certamente uma acao immoral e ilegal. Eu procurarei os danos.

I will be writing to the local congressman immediately. The removal of my intestines is surely and immoral and illegal action. I shall seek damages.

I slipped into the empty classroom next door.

I recognized the place. It was nothing shocking. I recognize every place, or think I do. I dream of them non-stop, I write about them endlessly. That's what I do, that's how I waste my life. So here it is, this is it.

Tom Piccirilli

My soul had been in a terrarium all the time, curled under some plant life, sitting on a toadstool. It glanced up as I entered, pale and shaky. It let out a tiny angry bleat as I reached down.

A security guard stepped up beside me. He gave me a slow and knowing grin, and I gave him one right back, a hip wink that said it all. Of course, it was Stevie Melton. My face was reflected in his shining badge and I could hardly believe I was the same person I was twenty minutes ago, two days ago, twenty years ago. My soul was restless and fidgety with strange, ugly, human needs.

I left. I hit the hall with my hands cupped around my soul, trying to protect it from enemies, miscreants, evildoers, lovers, ass-kissers, know-it-alls, my ghosts, my memories, the sharp edges of my wants and dreams. I got out to my dead brother's car. I leaned against the bumper until all the buses passed by, the kids' faces looking down at me, some smiling, most of them indifferent. The next time I checked, my hands weren't cupped any more, they were at my sides, and my soul was on the loose once more.

It was almost time to meet with Celeste Campion's cinema club. I was still a little shocked that she had known the titles of my early films, even if I had spoken to her drama class before and didn't remember doing it. I hardly mentioned the good stuff. I always focused on Zypho. Everyone wanted me to focus on Zypho and the later films, the horror flicks, the action pics, the low-budget crap that gave hope to every fledgling screenwriter, producer, and director. I inspired the shit out of fellow failures.

I knew her address. She lived less than a half mile from my ma. I used to play ball in the street there with a bunch of the other neighborhood kids.

I pulled up in front. There were a bunch of cars at the curb and in the driveway, skateboards, bikes, even a motorcycle. I walked up the drive to the garage. A side door was open and party noise erupted from within. I stepped inside, trying to tamp down the vague sense that I was doing something wrong. That I shouldn't be here without parental supervision. Their parental supervision, not mine.

The garage had been turned into a nice additional room. Celeste's dad would've had a good time cracking beers in here and watching sports with his buddies. He'd spent some cash on his man cave. Full sectional leather couches, love seats, a couple of recliners, widescreen TV, Blu-ray, the whole haul. No wonder his wife had put her stiletto heel down.

The club had hung up framed posters from some amazing films and cult classics. *Touch of Evil. Seven Samurai. The Third Man. The Wild Bunch. Re-Animator. Escape from New York. Glen or Glenda. Oldboy.* I didn't see Zypho anywhere and felt a slight pang of resentment. I hated that stupidass critter with all my being, but still, it had been my bread and butter for a while and remained my only claim to minor fame.

I was surprised at their numbers. They totaled close to twenty. I didn't think you could find that many kids who might actually appreciate cinema. They seemed evenly split among genders, races, and ethnicities. I had the feeling someone was performing a social experiment and running some kind of game on me. I waited for the beer and the pot to come out. It didn't happen. They passed around sodas. An Asian girl handed me something diet. I tried not to take it personally.

Celeste had picked up some pizzas on the way home from school. There was a wide variety, including a veggie lover's delight. I ate like I was at a cocktail party and moved among the group. Nobody appeared to find my presence odd. They chatted and I joined in where I could. They all wanted to have something to do with movies or stage. I gave them the names of agencies that I wasn't good enough to be represented by.

Eventually Celeste stood in front of the flat-screen and called the group to order. She actually said, "I'm calling the group to order."

She introduced me. She'd either Wikied me or was just that sharp that she knew a ton about my professional life. I was thankful she didn't know, or at least didn't say, anything about my personal cesspool. Laying it all out the way she did, I was ignited with a momentary surge of self-respect. It had been so long that I almost didn't realize what it was. My heart started moving along at a faster clip. I put my hand to my chest, thinking maybe this was it, I was having a coronary and they were going to lay me out on a slab of stone and cut out my heart with an onyx blade and let Eva cook it.

Celeste mentioned *Sleeping Where I Land, The Outlaw Light, The Way Down to Dream.* Whenever she said a title the group hooted and applauded. She got to Zypho and the gang went wild. They were kids. I forgave them. I didn't forgive myself or Monty. I didn't forgive the editor who'd re-cut the film to add in all the XXX action. I didn't forgive the guy with the ten-inch meatpole for doing unholy things to Zypho's nether regions.

They took it all seriously. They sat quietly like they were in class. They were attentive, accommodating, and alert. I took it seriously too. I knew my speech cold. I'd told it a hundred times before. I could talk the stars out of the sky. I had zip, earthiness, integrity, and numbers. I was still halfway worried that Mr. and Mrs. Campion might walk in at any time and think I was selling drugs or Ponzi scheming the children.

Then I took questions. This was always softer ground. There was a bigger chance to foul up. Certain questions got under my skin. I had difficulty responding to certain lines of thought. Welles kept looking down at me from *Touch of Evil.* I thought, Fuck you, fat man. I'm blazing full of light right now and you're smoking dirt. Don't give me those eyes that scream I'm wasting all my potential. I can make an ashtray like nobody else on wards six, seven, or eight. Nobody could ever knock me down in our gladiatorial matches. I still have both kidneys.

I made eye contact with Celeste. I played mostly to her and the other girls. It was human nature. I took questions. My scalp began to prickle.

WHAT MAKES YOU DIE

INNOCENT KID WHO HASN'T HAD HIS
LIVER TORN OUT AND STUCK ON A
PIKE YET:

Mr. Pic, some of your work is intensely stark and bleak, but it's
also surprisingly funny. How do
you manage to put so much empha-
sis on such spiritual pain and
have laughs along the way?

TOMMY PIC:

Because it can't be true to life
if it's just one aspect or the
other. Life is a tragi-comedy.
One facet underscores the other.
The funnier something is, the
more of a setup it is when the
bottom drops out. You get that?
When you hit bottom, it's the
perfect time to make a joke. You
ever see someone really lose it?
Someone who really slams into a
wall? He doesn't have any more
tears to cry, he just cuts loose
with laughter. In your darkest
hour you seem to find the punch
line to the grand joke.

PRETTY LITTLE LASS WHO GIVES ME
UNSAVORY THOUGHTS THAT I WILL
FOCUS ON MORE DEEPLY LATER ON
TONIGHT ALONE IN MY BEDROOM
WHILE GOD BLINDS ME FOR MY
GREATEST SINS:

Were you working out your worst
nightmare in *The Way Down to*

75

Dream or is it some kind of masochistic fantasy?

TOMMY PIC:

Both. When you get down to it, that's what all writers of any sort, whether screenwriters or prose writers or poets, are doing. Indulging in their fantasies. Horror and science fiction and so-called dark literary writers are indulging in their meanest, ugliest visions. Possibly so the audience doesn't have to. It's our duty and calling. We tear into our own scars and make them bleed to provide safety for our viewers, our readers, our fans, our lovers. And it's off that blood that we make our art. If it is art. ("It is," calls out the Asian cutie.) Well, whatever it is, we create it by invoking anguish and conflict and deep drama. Them's the movies, gang.

Applause, nods of agreement, slurping of pizza, someone moaning, "Ugh, mushrooms."

CELESTE CAMPION:

I don't want to get into any great debate on a controversial topic here, Mr. Pic, but it seems you take a stance on abortion in *The Outlaw Light*. The protagonist is haunted and guilt-ridden over a visit to

Planned Parenthood. Is that your intention, or did the director alter your goal, or am I simply reading into it?

TOMMY PIC (startled, recouping lost ground, squinting):

I'm definitely not taking a position. Even if I had one to take I don't think I would in that kind of a script. I just focus on one particularly distressing event and do what I do as a writer of dark material, which is share the pain. The protagonist in *The Outlaw Light*, marvelously portrayed by Fredrick Whitefield...

Applause for Fredrick Whitefield's marvelous portrayal.

TOMMY PIC (CON'T):

...the protagonist's marriage caused him pain, as did his career, and the economy. Losing his child, what might have been his child, caused him pain. Choosing not to have a child gives him pain. This was written as a thriller of sorts, a psychological suspense story. I'm not writing about butterflies and puppies.

Laughter and awws over butterflies and puppies. Judgmental sharp look from Orson Welles. Debased grin of Ed Wood.

TOMMY PIC (CON'T):

I'm choosing major life experiences and incidents. Significant matters of the heart.

> BOY IN A WIFE-BEATER T-SHIRT,
> MUSCULAR ARMS, NOSE RING,
> EYEBROW PIERCING, WISPY GOATEE,
> ALL THE THINGS THAT WOULD MAKE
> HIM A PRIMO PROSTITUTE ON SUNSET
> BOULEVARD WHILE THE LIMOUSINES
> LINED UP AT THE CURB:

In *Sleeping Where I Land*, there's a great bit of dialogue. Jensen Wright says, "This is the thing I will never be forgiven for. This is the moment God will point to with his burning hand at the hour of my death."

Nods and murmurs for either Jensen Wright's portrayal or the underage male prozzy's oration.

BOY PROZZY (CON'T):

You also mention such things as archangels with fiery swords. Did you mean to take any kind of a religious stance?

TOMMY PIC:

Oh fuck me, no.

Voluminous laughter and hoots for adult cursing in the presence of teens. Celeste's eyes checking the door to see if Mrs. Campion is hovering nearby. I check too. For Celeste's mother. For my mother.

TOMMY PIC (CON'T):

I'm talking about a personal relationship with fate. With the future. With death. The things that haunt you have weight and meaning and you carry them with you through life. They're a part of you. They give your existence form. When I say God is angry with me it's because I'm angry with me. It's the poetry of the anguish. As a lapsed Catholic, what else could I find as powerful as images of saints and martyrs and archangels? Of course that's all going to make it into the scripts. And from there into the movies. Sometimes. Sometimes not. Sometimes you're working with Neolithic asswipe directors who don't understand that the fucking picture he's making is coming from somewhere else, from someone else. He thinks it's coming from himself, from out of a burning bush, but it's born from the writer.

ASIAN GIRL WHO THINKS I'M FAT:

This might sound a little melodramatic, but is *Zypho, the*

*Critter from Beyond the Edge of
Space* your personal manifesto?

TOMMY PIC:

You're right, it sounds way too
melodramatic, kid.

ASIAN CHIPPIE:

The definition of "manifesto"
is—

TOMMY PIC:

I know what the goddamn definition of manifesto is.

ASIAN CHIPPIE:

For the other members of our
group who don't, it's a—

TOMMY PIC:

Everyone knows what a goddamn manifesto is. Is there anyone here who
doesn't know what a manifesto is?

Hands raise here and there.

TOMMY PIC (CON'T):

Man, our educational system really
is shit. That school was shit when
I went there, but it's gotta be
worse now. Do they still steal the
innards from the Portuguese punks?

WHAT MAKES YOU DIE

CELESTE CAMPION:

Excuse me? The Portuguese what?
Steal their what?

TOMMY PIC:

Forget it. Okay, so some of you
here don't know what a manifesto
is. (*Pointing to the Asian girl*). Go for it.

ASIAN CHIPPIE:

It's a written statement declaring
publicly the intentions, motives,
or views of an individual.

TOMMY PIC:

Right. I don't think I discuss my
intentions or motives, whatever
they might be, but you'll find
some of my views in the films,
even in Zypho, sure. I mean, I
have my moments when I would just
love to suck brain juice out of
young minds like yours with my
tentacles. (*Some laughter. Not enough.*) I
revisit my themes. I return to
the well of my inspiration. It's
what I have to do, especially now
that I'm older. My fears and pas-
sions and loves have shifted. The
things that used to scare me no
longer do. Things I never cared
about before now distract and
draw my attention. Zypho coming
down to do his thing, well, it's

an attack in the dark. We all fear that. It's the most natural thing in the world.

ASIAN CHIPPIE:

In the adult-rated version Zypho rapes women and lives off their vaginal fluids. Is this a commentary on the eternal battle between the sexes or is it simply a childishly perverse male fantasy?

TOMMY PIC (being fat, wanting another slice of pizza, scared that the vice squad is going to kick in the garage door and snap the cuffs on him just for being in the same room with underage kids who say the word 'vaginal,' wanting a drink, wishing one of these little fuckers would light up a bone, thinking maybe he ought to ask somebody to share their anti-anxiety meds, anybody got Percocet, Vicodin, some Xanax?):

Uhm. Ah. I didn't have anything to do with that particular edition of the film.

ASIAN CHIPPIE:

Is Zypho a confessional?

TOMMY PIC:

Since very little of it actually happened, I'd have to say no. It just feels like it might have happened. You know. If we were ever attacked by a critter from beyond the edge of space who happened to live off our brain juices, which, you know, I suppose could happen. Or you could take it as a metaphor. I think... I think I meant that... that it was supposed to be... ah...

ASIAN CHIPPIE (looking smarter and yummier by the minute):

By confessional, I mean—

TOMMY PIC:

I know what confessional means.

ASIAN CHIPPIE (yummified):

For the members of our group who—

TOMMY PIC:

Oh Jesus, come on, your buddies here know what confessional means, don't they?

A couple of hands raise around the room.

TOMMY PIC (CON'T):

Oh Jesus fuck!

OVERWEIGHT KID WITH THICK GLASSES AND AN ALREADY

RECEDING HAIRLINE WHO DOESN'T
HAVE A GODDAMN CHANCE IN THE
WORLD AND WILL DEFINITELY WIND
UP KILLING HIS OWN ASS IN SOME
SELF-ASPHYXIATION MASTURBATORY
SCREW UP:

Mr. Pic, what will your next
movie be?

TOMMY PIC:

It's called *What Makes You Die.*

A thirty second count as nothing more is said.

CELESTE CAMPION:

What's it about?

TOMMY PIC:

Uhm. Ahh, well. See. See, it's
about. It's about a girl in a box
and not in a bowl. There's a leg
in a bathtub and an old lady's
corpse on a roof. And there's
this dude called the Memento
Thief. He's interesting. He's
very interesting. I don't want to
ruin it for you. I'll get you all
tickets. You can attend the prem-
iere. With your parents' permis-
sion of course. You know.

KID DOOMED TO HANG HIMSELF IN
A CLOSET COVERED IN BABY OIL,
FORCING HIS MOTHER TO CLEAN UP

WHAT MAKES YOU DIE

HIS SELF-ASPHYXIATED SUICIDE,
HIDE ALL HIS S&M PORN DVDS AND
MAGAZINES, AND STUFF A CHICKEN
BONE DOWN HIS THROAT TO MAKE
IT SEEM LIKE AN ACCIDENT:

Would you do me the honor of
reading my script?

TOMMY PIC (taking a deep breath,
cooling jets, straining for sta-
bility, glancing over faces
again, remembering he's found
his soul, fighting for presence,
sensing sprinklings of goofer
dust (crematorium and grave)
about, looking toward Ed Wood
and thinking, by Christ, the
world laughed at him, but he
made movies):

You don't want that, kid. You
don't want whatever I've got
wiping off on your work.

CHICKEN BONE CHUCK:

I'd really value your opinion,
Mr. Pic.

TOMMY PIC:

And you shouldn't. Why should anything I have to say matter?
There's no secret here. There's no
grand mystery. You write the
script, you get an agent, or not,
you push to producers, you mail it
in over the transom, you flood

85

email boxes, you cut and run to
L.A., you work as wait staff for a
few years, maybe more, maybe less,
you get some kind words, you get
some criticisms, you rewrite, you
get your masterpiece redrafted as
a cartoon or a slasher film or a
karate flick. Your major dramatic
beats between father and son, best
friends, born enemies, first
loves, are downgraded to illegal
boxing clubs, prison boxing matches, CGI battles between robots.
Your autobiography will be turned
into a quest for vaginal or brain
juices. You live with it. You cry
about it. You cash the check. You
don't bother to keep your mantel
clear for Academy Awards anymore.
You try not to drink too much. You
don't give in to crack... too
much. You get tested for AIDS a
lot. Even if you're not getting
laid. And you won't be, trust me.
I wouldn't want to steal all that
experience from you, kid. You need
to live it for yourself. That's my
gift to you. That's my legacy.
You're my heir apparent. You,
Chuck, you—

CHUCK:

My name's not Chuck, it's—

TOMMY PIC:

—you, Chuck, are like my own
child, my son, and if I can

teach you anything at all about
family matters, about personal
perspective, about the depth of
feeling I have for you—

CHUCK:

I don't think I feel comfortable
about you discussing your depth
of feeling for me, Mr. Pic.

TOMMY PIC:

—it's that you should always
write from the heart no matter
how the work gets screwed with,
how it gets rearranged, re-
edited, redrafted, how different
it becomes because of invasive
editors, narrow-minded studio
execs, nimrod directors, the
nameless, faceless fuckers who
are brought in to ghost write
and "clean up" your work, the
yahoo middle Americana naiveté
and willfully ignorant who are
bussed in from fucking Oshkosh
to sit in on the test screenings
and purposefully, purposefully,
I'm telling you, criticize and
skew the film just because they
can, because they've been given
a hint of power in a world that
otherwise ignores their every
thought and whim and care and
dream and breath and life and
death. I've read those test
cards, and Mr. and Mrs. Front

Porch America don't know shit about what makes a good movie good or a shit one shit. Chuck, my wayward son—

CHUCK:

I'm not your son, Mr. Pic, wayward or otherwise. My name isn't Chuck. You don't look so good, sir. Would you like us to call a doctor or somebody?

TOM PIC:

Chuck, don't show anybody your script. Not your best friend, not your ma, not your sister Deb, not your cousin Jane—

CHUCK:

I don't have a sister Deb or a cousin Jane, Mr. Pic, my sister's name is—

TOM PIC:

—not your agent, who will ask you to clarify the role of the Memento Thief, who will tell you to bring the old man with only half a face and a shotgun back in for the third act. He'll ask who killed the mouse, he'll ask if the Memento Thief is in the house. He will ask about the old lady on the roof. And really, it's all there on

the page, it's got to be there
on the page, anyone who's
smelled goofer dust knows it,
anyone at all with a dragon
ghost in his guts will understand. Tony Todesco knows.
Kathy Lark gets it. Kathy puts
a cool hand to your warm head
and whispers that she thinks
the screenplay is perfect.
Don't show your script to anybody, Chuck, just leave it out
and let the dead fill their
cold, empty nights with it.

CELESTE CAMPION:

I think that's the perfect ending
point right there. Let's all
thank our special guest, Mr. Tom
Pic, for taking the time out of
his busy schedule and paying our
cinema appreciation club a visit.

Applause. Asian chippie looking at me like I'm a math problem she can't solve without exponential logarithms. Boy prostitute's mouth already slightly parted, waiting for the cock of Beverly Hills business-men and slick accountants for the drug cartels. Chuck's puzzled grimace. His throat bared, waiting for the rope.

I picked up a couple of pints of Jameson's from a nearby liquor store and sucked one down in the parking lot, keeping an eye out for the cops. After fifteen minutes my nerves began to steady. I went home, sat at the kitchen table while my ma discussed her day and my sister Deb ate dinner sloppily and tittered for no reason almost every time I spoke.

She found me funny. It was endearing and frustrating. I had an easily triggered gag reflex. Every time I looked over at her, with tomato sauce covering her face and macaroni tossed every which way around her corner of the table, I had to glance away quickly or feel my throat tighten.

The hospital bills were stacked on the kitchen counter, near the toaster. A one-week stay on the ward had been broken down among several different medical groups, health systems, MDs, psychiatrists, psychotherapists, ER attendants, ambulance drivers. All the tests had been collated. The mental ones, the physical ones, x-rays, stress tests, heart and reflex evaluations, blood tests, stomach-pumping. They had all recently decided that they didn't take my type of insurance anymore. The printouts reached numbers I could hardly fathom. Added together, it was tens of thousands. There were handwritten notes along the borders that I couldn't make out. There were red stamps everywhere telling me to pay immediately.

Gideon had left a Post-it stating: CHECK THE NEW YORK STATE INDIGENT PROGRAM.

My mother was telling me some convoluted shopping tale about my aunt Carmela, cousin Jane, and cousin Caroline. I didn't get it. I didn't want to get it. I kept looking up at her and going, "Is that right?" Every time I did, Deb laughed.

I folded the bills up and tried to stuff them into my pocket, but there were too many sheets. Together they were hard as rock and thick as a Tolstoy novel.

My mother paused and I said, "Oh yeah? That right?" She started up again.

I wondered how much I could bring in with my ashtray building skills. I wondered if there was a lucrative black market for babies in the bin.

"I've got some work I need to finish," I said.

"All right," my ma, my poor ma, still putting up with me, said.

I rushed down into the basement, making sure I locked the door behind me. I sat at my computer and laid out the screenplay pages and guzzled from the other pint. My eyes still couldn't stay focused on the screenplay. I said aloud to my other self, if there was another self, "So what do you need? Should I stick another knife in my belly or go out and buy a bottle of gin? You think you could tell me? I just want to help out here." And it was true, I did. I didn't mind moving out of the way, so long as the job could get done. So Monty could have a new script he was proud of, that he could sell, maybe for real money, maybe for more than that. Monty didn't give a heave-ho for artistic expression or critical success, but I did. Maybe I did. Somewhere deep under the dragon.

I did what I did best. I watched movies. I popped in DVD after DVD. I listened to commentaries late into the night. I kept drinking. I thought of Eva, of Trudy, of Celeste, the Asian chippie, Orson Welles' ex-wives. I put in the dirty version of Zypho and tried to get myself horny enough to feel the need to yank the weasel, but it just wasn't happening. The liquor flowed through me, easing up my muscles, my loud mind, my crazed memories, my endless embarrassments, and I could sense sleep coming. I wondered if the other me would come along with it. I wondered if my body would go to keyboard without me and finish the script. What a blessing that would be. To write something people wanted that I didn't have to suffer over, didn't have to sweat or cry across. I held up the last sip from the pint bottle and toasted him. Go get 'em, killer.

When I woke it was raining plastic-sole footsteps. They drummed into my hangover and proved I was still alive.

I glanced over at the computer desk. There were no extra pages of the script up on the screen. Nothing had been printed out. Nothing had been emailed. The other me hadn't done his thing. Maybe he was waiting for yet a different other me to take the reins and the responsibilities that we couldn't handle. It sounded perfectly plausible. I could imagine there being ten thousand mes inside my bones and blood, all meeting with cinema appreciation clubs, digging dragons out of their bellies, hoping to clarify the Memento Thief.

The running upstairs continued. It meant my cousins Jane and Caroline were here. It meant they'd brought their kids. Every so often one of the children would try the basement door and give a thump. I heard my name called out.

My stomach growled. Aunt Carmela would have stopped off for fresh bagels and donuts. Grandma would be up there talking in Italian about her bingo winnings, tomato plants, and the Mets. Someone would have put a DVD on for the kids and the kids would be ignoring it, running out the front door, around the yard, and in through the side door. Along the way they'd run down the stone steps to the cellar door and give it a kick. It sounded like we were being invaded by a tribe of pygmies.

I rolled over in bed and buried my face. There were taps at the windows. They were leaning down, calling my name. "Tom? Tom? Are you in there? Tom, what are you doing?"

I thought I knew their names, but whenever I talked to one, or asked one if it was Dylan or Emily or Alicia, I got no response or the wrong response, and I wasn't sure if they were just fucking with me or not.

"Tom? Are you watching a movie? What movie are you watching? Can we watch too?"

I lifted my head from my pillow. "What's your name?" I asked.

"You know my name!"

"No, I really don't."

A burst of giggles. "You're silly!"

"I am silly!" I said. I was silly.

I showered, shaved, gargled, and stared in the mirror, trying to go deep into my own eyes and meet myself half-way inside there. I had things to tell me. I wasn't sure what to start with. I didn't know if I really wanted to listen. I glared and the mirror glared back.

I went up and my grandmother had the baby on her lap. I still didn't know who the kid belonged to. Caroline and Jane seemed to trade off. They took care of the kids en masse. They shouted orders almost indiscriminately. My mother steered clear, mostly. Aunt Carmela kept them happy by feeding them too much sugar. Whenever one kid ran within reach she'd jam a donut at it. They'd come and stand next to me and say something I didn't understand and then run away laughing.

WHAT MAKES YOU DIE

Jane, Caroline, my ma, Aunt Carmela, and Grandma made small talk with me and each other. They were used to me going in and out of the hospital. It wasn't a big thing anymore. It didn't deserve a lot of tiptoeing. Grandma would mutter prayers under her breath for me. She'd stick little statues of saints on the dining room table, and the little things would stare at me with flaming hearts and halos and covered in tiny birds and all kinds of wacky stuff that brought up my Catholic guilt. She'd reach out with her small, powerful hand, a hand that had worked in factories in the 40s to help battle the Axis powers, and pat my arm. I didn't know if she had been a riveter, but she could've been. She was strong and I was weak. The saints glared at me with disdain.

A child ran up. "You're weird!"

"I am weird!" I agreed. I was weird.

It went on like that. The baby kept holding its arms out to me and trying to crawl free from Grandma's lap. Eventually she lifted the kid like a football and passed it off to me. It clapped giddily. I still couldn't tell if it was a boy or a girl or whose it was or what it was called. Nobody seemed to use names. Jane and Caroline just shouted out orders to the troops. "Stop running! Come in and get yourselves cleaned up! What is that? What are you doing? Leave it alone! Put it down! Do you want juice? Come drink your juice!"

The baby went, "La la la la la la la la la."

It sounded like fun so I tried it. I went, "La la la la la la la la la," and the baby went wild. It squealed and squeaked and tried to grab my face with both its chubby hands. I lalaed some more and it went bananas and all the ladies came closer and both Caroline and Jane whipped out their phones and took photos of it.

The baby clapped and grinned and was beautiful and un-scarred by the world. I clapped and grinned. It shit its pants. I held it away from me like a leper and Aunt Carmela scooped it up like a lateral pass.

I retreated back to the basement.

I called Eva and caught her at a bad time while she had a run of customers at the store. She rattled off her address and I wrote it down and promised to see her Friday.

The rest of the week burned by. I tried to read the screenplay and couldn't. I tried to fake a new scene based on Monty's notes and couldn't. I searched through every file and flash drive I had looking for the script and couldn't find it anywhere. I stared at the screen and fought through my memory, hunting for characters or dialogue or images. They weren't there.

I checked the mirror again and tried and call down to the other me and make him come through for us.

My mother made meals and I ate them and listened to her talk about whatever the hell she was talking about, and I failed to respond properly. My sister laughed whenever I botched a conversation. In her own way, Deb was sharper than me, more focused. The polkas went on and on and, Christ save me, I was starting to like them.

I watched a lot of movies. I had the vague sense that I could relearn everything I'd forgotten about myself and my love of writing and my need to express myself on the cold, empty, bloodless page. I kept thinking that if I could just run across the right bit of dialogue, one special scene or frame of film, then everything else would come back to me. Like so many folks, I just wanted to find out exactly where things had derailed so I could go back and get it right a second time.

Every day the family came by and the kids ran around like maniacs—and I knew what maniacs running around looked like. The baby sat on my lap and I lalalaed with it. I read the books that Eva had bought me and tried to reach backward through time to the teenager I'd been who'd burned to run off to Hollywood and make films and meet his heroes and gaze wide-eyed at the stars filling their Hummers at gas stations and eating lunch at local establishments like normal people ate at local establishments. Getting drunk and with cheese and sauce tucked into the corners of their mouths.

Monty called and asked about the pages. I told him they were coming along. He asked what I thought about his notes. I told him they were thoughtful and to the point. I thanked him profusely for helping to make the screenplay even better. He sounded chipper. He was doing well in New York and finally making some money. He had decided to splurge a little and said he'd send a limo for me on Monday at six a.m. to catch a flight out of Kennedy to L.A. He'd meet me at the gate. He sounded more enthusiastic than I'd heard him in years. He had a few meetings set up already. He mentioned names. Some of them were big guns, some of them were nobodies. Monty was playing the entire board, which was why he always managed to keep his head above.

The kids banged around upstairs. They ran to the basement windows, bent and peered in at me. They said, "Hi, Tom!"

"Don't forget me," I told them.

"We won't," they said, and giggled and rushed off again.

Eva didn't live in Manhattan, but in Hoboken, New Jersey. I drove my dead brother Bobby's car, following the directions over to Jersey. I got nervous driving in the city at night, through the Lincoln Tunnel, thinking about Bobby constantly bitching at me for getting grime and dust on his car. His voice was so loud it sounded like he was sitting in the back seat leaning forward.

Eva rented out a nice-sized, freshly-painted house with a well-kept little lawn in a newly gentrified bedroom community. The punk rock Gothy roommate answered the door when I knocked, and said, "My name's Darla. I don't recognize you so you must be a friend of Eva's. If you're not and you're just crashing, I don't care about that either. Just come in and have some fun."

She sounded like she was straining to be bohemian, so I just smiled and stepped inside. I brushed shoulders with a couple dozen folks, all of them younger than me. I found the bar and poured myself three fingers of bourbon. It was top-shelf liquor.

I circled the crowd and the cliques and the clusters and the wallflowers. I discovered Eva playing a proper hostess in the kitchen, pouring bowls of chips and salsa while Darla baked hors d'oeuvres and put together finger sandwiches. I was suddenly embarrassed to have so much liquor in my glass, but not so embarrassed to suck it down in a half second flat. I shoved the empty glass away from me on the counter.

Eva wore a short black dress with a matching suede jacket. She was sexy as hell. I was sorry I couldn't see her armband tattoo, but I grooved on staring at her bare legs. They were shapely and muscular and I took notice of her knees. They were very attractive knees. I don't think I had ever given a damn about someone's knees before, but there it was.

Her hair was still in a ponytail. As she tossed her head side to side, the ponytail followed with great velocity, brushing against her chin. I wanted to ask her a thousand questions that she'd always answer with "no." I wanted to see her shake her head, the hair bobbing left and right. It was the kind of small thing that could turn a man on forever, give him strength when he needed, or just drive him nuts.

She spotted me and said, "Hey!"

"Hi, can I do anything to help?"

My ma had taught me right, as right as she could. Always ask to help out in the kitchen.

"Taste this," Darla said, and pressed some kind of baconed-cheese thingie hors d'oeuvres at me. I swallowed it in two bites and declared, "Delicious."

It was the right thing to say. It was always the right thing to say. Women who spent any time at all cooking, even if it just meant tossing cheese dip in the microwave, wanted some kind of respect and gratitude for it. "Thank you!"

Darla grabbed a couple of trays waitress-style and backed out the kitchen door. Eva handed me a bowl and said, "Could you carry this?"

"Sure."

She leaned in so close her belly almost touched mine. Gideon hissed his hatred from before the age of man. I took the bowl and held it against my stomach tightly as if to shut him up. Eva smiled. She took a chip, ran it through the dip, and popped it into my mouth. I chewed and said, "Good."

I followed her out into the house. We placed the bowls on the coffee table in front of a group of drunk frat boys staring at the widescreen HDTV, watching the DVD of a Shaw Brothers martial arts film. I recognized Chen Kwan Tai and Lo Lieh doing some slick kung fu from a flick from the late 70s. The guys were laughing their balls off. It got under my skin. I turned and said, "*Executioners from Shaolin*. A classic."

"This idiotic bullshit?" one kid asked.

I wanted to chop him in the throat. I wanted to box him up in a crate and mail him to Hong Kong and have him say that in front of a nation that would beat his ass raw with bamboo sticks.

Eva put her hand on my back the way my wife used to do, giving a little push, a "get out there and give it a go" motivational gesture.

She said, "Mingle for a bit. I'll be right back."

"Right."

The other Wiccans were on a couple of futons in a sunroom at the back of the house, holding court to a neo-gothic bunch sitting on the floor wearing leather, white pancake mix, black lipstick, and contact lenses to make them look like androgynous movie vampires. They looked Hollywood good. Only the most alienated could form such a tight and conformed clique. If you tried to say hello they might chop you to pieces, they had razors under their tongues. They showed them off. They were tattooed with spider webs, twining roses, ravens on their necks and wrists. I couldn't help myself and began to drift over. I thought I might have a thing for girls who looked dead.

Darla hung with them but didn't seem to be too tight with the gang. The punk rocker in her must've had a fierce independent spirit that didn't want to make nice with the emo mooks.

Wands of eucalyptus incense add a sweet and cloying perfume to Eva's place. The white witches were a married post-op transgendered couple named Asriel and Mova. They were in full regalia tonight: ebony robes and about twelve pounds of silver jewelry clanging around their necks. Pentacles, sun wheels, pendants with Latin phrases scrawled across their broad faces. If they bought all that shit from Weird Sisters, then no wonder Eva's store was making serious bread.

The emo-gothic-zombie kids were alert, listening raptly. A fawn-colored pug was lying in the foyer on its side, eyes open but snoring loudly. At least it wasn't a black cat. The curve of its pudgy belly quivered with each breath, and the dog eyed me suspiciously. Out in the den, the HDTV blared in Cantonese. I knew exactly what scene *Executioners from Shaolin* it was.

The dead chicks paid me no attention, and I felt a little humbled by their indifference. Sometimes you could get shot down before they even glanced at you.

I found the bourbon again and poured another three fingers. I sucked it down as fast as possible and filled the glass once more. I sipped, waiting for relief, but it wasn't there and it didn't feel like it was coming. I kept catching snatches of conversation like a radio tuner spinning around and around and never settling anywhere. The cold sweat began to run down my neck. I went on the hunt for Eva, searching room by room, but couldn't find her. It didn't take much to shake my faith in reality or my own history. I knew hysterics in the hospital who'd dreamed up entire families for themselves. Wives, kids, pets. You'd have to play along or watch them throw a fit.

I wondered, Is that what I'm doing here? Is Eva just in my head?

I wanted to ask the ghost of the Pleistocene Age Komodo dragon from the island of Gili Dasami, whose bones were showcased at the Queensland Museum, "Gideon, is she real or did I just dream her up?"

One of the frat guys—burly in a gray college sweatshirt with the sleeves torn off, crushed corn chips sticking to his wet neck—looks up and said to me, "Someone's looking for you."

"Who?"

"I don't know."

"You sure they wanted me?"

"Yeah."

"How do you know?"

"What?"

"I've never met you. How do you know me?"

"You're the weirdo who's wandering around all alone and hasn't said a word to anyone all night."

Our dialogue ended as if a guillotine had come down. A tension in the air picked up and occupied the room.

I slammed down my drink, found the bar, made another. I looked for Eva. She was nowhere in sight. I smelled trap. I always smelled trap. My head ran to B movie plot lines of women who wanted to dispatch men for their heinous ways.

I looked over at the pug, who watched me carefully. The dog's lip curled in a sneer. He had a tag hanging from his collar. Pyewacket.

It almost got a smile from me. That was the name of the witch's familiar in the movie *Bell, Book, and Candle*. I liked inside jokes so long as I got them.

My edginess kept growing. Eva didn't return. I got worried. Not worried about me standing around being lonely worried, but dangerously worried. Like perhaps something had happened to her, assuming she existed at all. I started asking folks, "You seen Eva?" No one had. No one admitted it.

The B movie soundtrack started up in my head. A cool jazz-o drum riff denoting action and suspense in classic film noir. I started actively hunting through the rooms for her. The place was bigger than I'd thought. All places in movies were bigger than the protagonist thought because he had to wander around like a dipshit for a while, walking into broom closets and pantries before he got a chance to either do heroic things or get his face blown off by a shotgun.

Pyewacket clambered to his feet and snuffled his way over to a redhead standing with a brunette and a blonde. In a script that's all that you'd need to describe them because that would be the sum total of their existence in the story—to simply be the redhead, the blonde, or the brunette. The redhead looked down at the dog and broke into a luscious laughter. She bent and made baby faces at him, saying, "Oh look! He's so ugly he's absolutely adorable."

Pye froze in shock, like somebody'd just threatened to have him neutered. A whine broke from his throat—it was the same noise I made whenever a woman turned me down on the dance floor. Pye blinked and cocked his head, snarled, and lunged for the girl's throat.

Thank Christ he was only a pug and had no real snout, just this blunt mouth with tiny, ineffective teeth, slobbering against her cleavage. Sort of a turn-on, in that disgusting under-the-counter-man-the-Asian-market-is-especially-freakish porno sort of way. The redhead flung her drink in the air, and her two friends started waving their hands about their faces, helplessly prancing in circles.

I rushed over, grabbed Pye in midair, and sort of waltzed him out of the room.

Asriel and Mova were in the middle of chanting, "...*here there be forces beyond the kith of men*...." It sounded about right. The emo-Goth kids were damn near quivering with excitement, nerve-wracked and waiting for dark magic to crash through the roof and swallow their commonplace lives. Hellspawn generals wore velvet blouses; just ask any of these kids.

They could sense the bowels of hell opening up just for them. So could I, maybe. I wondered if Kathy could when it had happened to her, if it had happened to her.

They thought it might be fun to fuck on a grave and have skeletal hands come out of the ground and drag them down into the mud. As if somehow death might actually make them *better* than everybody else. We all needed a dream.

If any of them actually saw the inside of the ICU ward they'd shit themselves and run for Mama's apron. When I was brought into the ER to dry out and left in the mental wings of hospitals I used to drunkenly shamble around and visit the other wards. Cancer victims coughing up their own lungs. The humming, beeping, ticking, and endless buzzing of machines that breathed for the ill and the elderly. Checking out the brain scans that graphed your thoughts and lack of consciousness, the gray tumors that chewed their way through the raw egg of your brain. Cysts that crawled down the sterile hallways, looking for a chest cavity to call home.

For some reason I've given Pyewacket a voice. It was strangely similar to my former classmate Stevie Melton's, the security guard at the high school. I could picture my lady shrink tick off six or seven reasons why that might be, and she'd be wrong about all of them.

"Put me down," Pye said.

"Don't bite the ladies, Pyewacket. You'll get us both in trouble."

I carried him to the back door and out into a tiny back yard where other partygoers were drinking and talking. I still couldn't find Eva.

The moon sliced through a wedge of adjacent buildings and houses. A storm brewed in the air, sooty clouds rolled against silver, tussling in the night sky.

There was a heaviness in my chest, maybe the alcohol, maybe my ghosts, maybe the human need to find my hostess.

"I asked you to put me down," Pye said.

"Sorry."

I dropped the pug and watched him saunter along the fence, pissing on dead leaves cluttering the slats. I wished that I smoked. I wanted to light a cigarette and let the flame flare in the darkness, illuminating my face, because the film was still rolling on in my mind.

I turned and looked back through the window and saw Asriel and Mova slitting open their palms and letting their blood drip into an ornate goblet. The cup appeared to be ancient, as if it had sat in the dining halls of hoary kings. I moved across the weed-strewn lawn to the window to get a better look. Midget skulls encircled the base, and the handle was embellished and crafted from metal bodies twining together. Diminutive faces contorted in agony and perverse pleasure. Amazing what you could pick up on eBay for twenty bucks plus shipping.

The knife they used in the ritual was a dagger rimmed with fake jewels. Glass opals, emeralds, and rubies reflected the vapid expressions of the adoring Goth punks who couldn't wait to get their lips on the goblet. I knew one thing. They hadn't bought the blade at the Weird Sisters shop. I'd looked at those knives and they were the real deal.

As the dagger was passed around, the kids' eyes ignited with the dream of alchemy, as if this were the only way to find God, any god at all. They each poked their palms and oohed and aahed as a drop or two welled and spilled into the cup.

One leather-deather was done up in a black duster with a well-groomed devil's Vandyke, wearing fake fangs he'd had specially made by his dentist. He was about to burst into tears because he couldn't bring himself to cut his own skin. Maybe that made him saner than everybody else. I could remember the feeling of tearing at my own flesh as I tried to perform hara-kiri. I liked that someone else was caught up in the role of a bloodletter but couldn't actually go through with it.

Mova moved to the guy, rubbed his back, spoke calming words the way any good witch should. Vandyke was still struggling to puncture his flesh. He was one of the old school Goths, pushing forty with threads of white working through his widow's peak, and he'd never gone near a tattoo shop or piercing parlor. The tears plummeted down his cheeks and hung in the waxed, properly curled ends of his mustache. His collar was dark with sweat and dusted with salt.

The dead kids were caught up in the action. So was I. So was Pyewacket, who sat nearby, watching. I grimaced thinking about the swill of inherent disease in the goblet. The recessed genes, flakes of black nail polish, the STDs, the genetic predisposition toward gloss and lace, the stupidity, the twisted helix defining the sisterhood of pain and brotherhood of anguish.

Pye said in my head, "These are some seriously goofy people."

I nodded. I had no right to nod, but I nodded anyway.

"She's calling you."

"What?"

"Over there. Behind you. In the yard."

"Oh Christ. Who is it?"

"Go on."

So I went. Eva stood by a small flower garden, luminescent, luxurious, star white, and lovely. She looked like a nice girl, as my grandmother would say, as my ma would say.

She attended me. "Are you having a good time?"

I put the question to the test and discovered that, after all, I was having a good time. It was better than sitting at home in the basement or watching the catatonics ferment on the ward. The booze was top shelf. The other revelers were entertaining, even if it was only because I was rewriting their parts as I went along. It was something to do.

"Yes, I am."

"I'm glad."

She put her hand out and, without touching me, moved it around my chest, my chin, my cheeks. "Your aura is blazing."

"Is that a good thing?"

She almost lied to me, but then thought better of it. "Not really."

"Oh."

And that was why I needed a cigarette. To take a puff, spend an extra second to come back with the perfect film noir line and rip it out there like Bogie might.

"You've been drinking a lot."

"Yes."

"Because it's a party?"

"Because I'm a binge drunk alcoholic."

"Then please don't have any more liquor tonight."

"I'll try."

I wondered if this was only a dream made real by the force of my own will—it's happened like that on occasion. You can sometimes find what you're looking for if you're hunting for the right thing. Usually I'm not, which is probably what brought me to a party in Hoboken to chat with a talking pug.

The wind wove and braided around her. She'd loosened her hair from the ponytail and it wafted and coiled about. Nearby conversations carried like fog that wrapped about us. It was cold enough that I could see her breath. It gently swirled and broke against my chin.

"You said you could help me." I gestured toward the window. "You're not going to have to bleed me into a goblet, are you?"

"I'm almost sure I won't need to do that. Almost."

I smiled. Maybe it was an honest smile. Sometimes it felt like one and then turned out to be some kind of leer that terrified people.

"I heard Pyewacket talking to me."

"What did he say?"

"Mostly negative things."

"In whose voice?" she asked.

"A guy I went to high school with. He's a security guard there now, at the school. It never let him go. He was never able to leave."

"You left."

"I just went back. I thought I'd lost my soul there. I went looking for it."

"Did you find it?"

"Yes. In a utility closet."

"Consider that a positive. Your talent and skill took you into a very difficult field and you succeeded at it. You're not that guy you went to school with."

"You sure do take things in stride," I said.

"I have a low threshold for boredom and normality."

"I guess you do."

She cocked her chin at me. I hadn't noticed before, but she had a drink in her hand. Something fruity and colorful. I wanted to kiss her again. I wondered what my father would have thought of her. I wondered what her brimstone-preaching gay meth-addicted father would have thought of me.

I said, "I don't think your white witch friends are going to be able to guide me toward peace."

"Why?"

"Because they seem like goofball frauds to me. Pyewacket agrees with me on that count, by the way."

She smiled. Her face glowed in the moonlight. "You don't respond to them."

"Not from what I saw."

"There are other people here tonight, Tom. Fascinating people. Some are writers. If you just tried to join in with a conversation you might like talking with them."

"I doubt that. Most writers don't talk about writing. It's boring. It would be like listening to a bricklayer talk about mixing mortar."

"Maybe that would be interesting?"

"Hell no."

She took a breath to respond to me but I was suddenly desperate to keep talking. "Eva, I don't think I ever thanked you for your gift the other day. For the books."

"You did thank me."

"Well, I don't think I thanked you enough. It meant a lot. Having lunch. Walking and talking with you. I appreciate it."

"It meant a lot to me too. I liked spending time with you."

Gideon hissed again. I remembered his note. I checked my watch. It was eleven. If anybody was going to cook my heart by midnight they were going to have to make a move soon. A part of me wanted them to try. I'd learned a thing or two in gladiatorial combat on the ward. I could hold my own against punks with razors under their tongues.

"You carry ghosts," she said. "I don't think I was clear enough in the city. We all do. It's a part of who we are, who we all are. You're just more aware. Like me, you see and understand things not everyone else does. Mediums call it being sensitive."

"So does my mother. And my agent."

"You're highly empathic and sympathetic and imaginative. Most of the time that causes us pain. That pain can send us into a spiral. And then—"

"Then?"

"Then our frustrations grow, our failures mount. We self-medicate. And we need help. Doctors. Therapists."

I was very aware of the smell of my own breath. "You keep saying 'we' but—"

"You don't think I understand about disappointment and loss?"

"I didn't say that."

"No, you didn't."

We stared into each other's eyes. Hers burned with the silver sky. I had a very strange feeling of total relaxation, the kind you couldn't get from anti-anxiety meds or antidepressants or primal scream therapy or a bottle of tequila or even plain old exhaustion. It was just the slight feeling of putting down a heavy weight that you didn't want to carry anymore, even if you picked it up in a minute or an hour from now.

"What do you need?" she asked.

"I need a lot of things."

"No, you don't."

"No?"

"No," she said with certainty. "There's one thing you feel would help you more than everything else."

"Do I?"

"Yes. What is it?"

I wondered. She wrapped her arm around mine again and we walked arm in arm across the yard to a couple of Adirondack chairs. It was chilly out and she wasn't dressed for it. I sat, and as she went to sit in the chair beside me I pulled her, gently, more gently than perhaps I'd ever done anything in my screwy life, and pulled her down on top of me. She slid into a perfectly comfortable position in my arms and we sat like that. I thought about her question.

I wondered. I wondered if I just needed to get laid. If I slept with her tonight, would that be what brought me back from my madness and depression and fear? Would I be able to get a factory job in Hoboken or Newark and accept my fate? Ten million other guys did it. Did I need to marry her? Did we need a pretty little house like this without a punk rock roommate or mothers-in-law in the attic? It might be enough. It was certainly a dream.

Or did I just need to somehow finish the script? Would it get me back to work as a functioning, semi-successful, even barely successful screenwriter in Hollywood, and would that be enough for me finally? Or was I wrong and did I really need Asriel and Mova to prick my thumbs and do the voodoo that they dood and give me some kind of spiritual cleansing that would make my soul pure as the driven snow?

Eva waited. I waited and wondered. I thought about my ex-wife. I'd driven her batshit too. Maybe all I needed to do was apologize to her and the ghost chasers, those poor bastards. Maybe paying for a full-time nurse for my sister so my mother could make some kind of an attempt at freedom and happiness without being hampered by her kids. Maybe if I parked my brother's car on his grave everything would fall back into place. Maybe if I figured out whose baby had been brought to the bin. I had my soul again, but it hadn't done me any good so far. Cutting the Komodo dragon out of my belly might be a start, but I'd flopped on doing that once already. So what was the next piece of the puzzle? What did I need?

Eva's hair flicked down across my face, dancing on the breeze, pecking my cheek and throat like she was kissing me, and then I realized that she was. I brought my mouth to hers and we kissed, the salt and the sugar meeting at last, the whiskey and the fruit, the godless and the goddess.

The answer wasn't much of an answer. It had been there since the beginning. It was the only answer. And it would always be beyond reach. I knew what to tell her. We kissed more passionately. We twisted in each other's arms. We were in the dark but there were people around doing their thing, drinking, talking. She undid my pants and I reached under her hem and pulled her panties aside and we fucked silently but kissing deeply. I hadn't been with a woman in more than two years, since meeting Trudy and the spider monkey at the Christmas party.

It was midnight. I was smitten. Maybe my heart was being cooked and eaten. Maybe that's what love was.

Afterward, nuzzling Eva, my forehead pressed to hers, breathing in her breath, I said, "I need to find Kathy Lark."

It was still dark when I woke in Eva's bed, with her naked and sleeping beside me, and the talking pug staring at me from the foot of the bed.

I checked my watch. It was three in the morning.

I glanced over and said, "Hello, Pye."

Pye didn't respond, which was probably a good thing. Either he was keeping his magic under rein or I was happier and more balanced and the depression had lifted a tad and I wasn't hallucinating quite as badly. In any case, I was glad I didn't have to hear Stevie Melton's voice so early in the morning.

An orange glow flickered against the window. I looked out in the yard and saw they had a pyre lit against what they used to call a coven tree. It was a small pyre. It was a small tree. From what I'd read in the books in Weird Sisters, it had to rise from the direct center of the covenstead, that area where witches drew the bulk of their power from, the place where natural earth energy emanated from and was at its strongest. I never would've expected a covenstead in Hoboken, but whatever. The fire consumed kindling, some crummy wooden trash, a ladder-back chair, an old kitchen cabinet, and other junk.

The window was open a crack. I thought I caught a whiff of blood. They were out there with the redhead that Pyewacket had made his move on. She was being bound to the coven tree with yellow nylon rope. She was laughing. She was very drunk. I could see that from here. The blonde and the brunette were in the group with the others, maybe twenty of them now, some performing ritual actions, raising their daggers, some just making signs in the air like they were at a heavy metal concert. Cheap daggers, but still sharp enough to cut. I wondered how fucked these people were. Not enough to really hurt someone, right? I wanted to call to Eva, but she looked so beautiful asleep, stretched across her sheets, with the orange glow flickering across the bed, that I didn't want to wake her.

The redhead thrashed a little. Vandyke and the others had a good grip on her and she flailed uselessly, the micro-skirt rearing to show off a sweet thong. Mova squawked and threw an arm over his eyes like the chick had flashed a crucifix. A couple of the frat boys stood around drunkenly gawking, holding their beer cans tight to their bellies and giggling quietly to one another. Darla was nowhere to be seen.

Mova and Asriel stripped out of their robes and beneath they had on some kind of ancient Celtic outfits now, looking half-fey, half-Cormac Mac Art. Their cheeks were rouged to a high varnish waxiness; the fire reflected so deeply in them that it looked like their faces were on fire.

The blonde said, "Hey, what's happening? What are you guys doing to Bethany?"

The brunette said, "Uhm, I think I'm gonna be sick..."

There were times when you called down the wrath of fate by not looking just a little farther to the left. Or taking the time to check under the bed for the dwarf holding a scythe, waiting to cut you down at the ankles. Or looking in the closet to see if her crazed lesbian lover was in there with a garrote. There were times when you damned yourself for not doing anything. For not saying a word. For not so much as coughing and announcing your presence.

Tom Piccirilli

"Bethany? Are you all right?"

"I want to go home!"

The tension in the yard kept building. Some of it was mine, left over from making love to Eva. The guys were chanting, "Take it off, take it off..." The witches were chanting something else entirely. The Goth kids' razor blades kept reflecting the blaze whenever they smiled. Hoboken, I thought. Who the hell knew you could get away with starting fires in your back yard in Hoboken? The drunk redhead threw up at the foot of the tree. The blonde and the brunette were trying to untie her but the punks were sort of dancing and wrestling with them and the air stank of sexual repression and an eagerness toward violence. I was very familiar with the stink of sexual repression and eagerness toward violence.

I stood there in the shadows, the fire occasionally flashing its light across me as the breeze shifted. The dead chicks glanced over. The redhead's vomit dripped form her chin as she struggled to free herself from her bonds. Punks tossed more shit on the pyre. It grew. Something in me grew with it.

I opened the window. I set my arms against the sill. My blood burned through me. My veins stood out, black and twisted along my arms. The muscles in my throat were like carved stone. Names were power. My name was Tommy Pic. Most of the time I hated it. A lot of people hated it. But it was mine. I stood alone at this hour, on this night, in this place, with my name.

I didn't cough or yell. I didn't shout or curse. I didn't smile or frown. I didn't make demands or offer promises. I didn't call on gods or men or demons of the infernal order.

I said, "Party's over."

They untied the redhead. They cleaned up their beer cans scattered in the weeds. They broke apart into their little groups and then into smaller groups and then they separated. Some walked back inside and some stepped out the little gate in the back fence. The fire burned for a while longer, and then it abruptly went out. The moon bathed me before I turned back to the bed and climbed in.

Eva rolled over and put her arms around me.

"What's that?" she murmured sleepily.

"What's what?"

"You were whistling. What's that song?"

"The Beer Barrel Polka."

"I like it, Tom. And I like you, too."

She kissed me. I kissed her back until we were panting. Then I said, "My name is Tommy."

We slept until dawn, got up before the sun broke, and stared into each other's eyes for a long while. "Do you want to make love again?" she asked. I pressed my mouth to her arm-band tattoo and tried to read the script written there but still couldn't make out the words.

"As a matter of fact, I would."

We moved together with a primal grace like a ballet we'd practiced and performed many times before. We laughed a lot. It was a good, deep, intensely happy laughter under the blankets and on top of them, on the bed and on the floor, and I felt like I had risen from the murky depths to meet her on the surface of a lake, clouds of mist in her hair.

Afterward, we took a shower together, and she dried me off and I dried her off. I dressed and slipped out of her room, thinking I might make us breakfast in bed, or at least pour us a couple bowls of cereal.

Pyewacket rose from the corner of the couch. I was startled to see the entire house cleaned up as if there'd never been a party at all. There weren't any bottles around, dirty glasses, bowls of munchies or dip. There wasn't a cushion out of place, not a dirty plate in the kitchen, not even in the sink. Pye followed me around. I checked the dishwasher. It was empty. I checked the cupboards. All the plates and bowls were there. I looked in the kitchen trash container. It was empty with a fresh bag. The fridge was well stocked.

Darla must've really been a type-A personality, or maybe the other me had been sleepwalking and cleaning up for the hell of it. I opened the DVD player to see if *Executioners from Shaolin* was still in there but it wasn't.

I said to the dog, "What about it, Pye? Was there a party here last night? Or was I dreaming it? Or am I dreaming this?"

The pug gave me a quizzical head ratchet but said nothing.

I walked back to the bedroom. Eva was putting lotion on the underside of her legs. She said, "What's the matter?"

"Nothing."

"You look a little upset."

"Just wondered if you wanted me to make you something for breakfast. Eggs? Pancakes?"

"You can make pancakes?"

"My mother's the best cook in the world. I learned from her."

"I wish I had the time, but I'm running a little late."

"Did you at least have fun throwing off your schedule?"

"I had a great deal of fun." She swept her hair aside and tied it back into her ponytail. "But I wanted to ask you, Tommy... did you write this?"

"Write what?"

"On my laptop."

She put the top back on her bottle of lotion and moved to her desk. She read the title carefully, slowly, maybe a touch fearfully. "*What Makes You Die. Act II.* It's been printed out. There's forty, no, almost forty-five pages here."

I didn't know how to answer. Whatever I said would be a lie. I probably did write them. But it wasn't me. Not this me. If there was any difference. Perhaps there wasn't. Maybe it wasn't me at all. Maybe it was my father. He'd loved movies. Maybe someone else. The gods might've taken pity. The infernal order might be playing more games with me. Pyewacket might've jumped up there and tapped away with his little paws. It all seemed as possible as it was impossible.

"Yes, I did," I said, trying to keep my voice firm.

"Forty-five pages? Last night? When? I didn't hear you at all. The printer's old and it's loud."

"When your friends were burning a pyre next to the

coven tree while the drunk redhead was being tied up and being prepared for sacrifice."

"What?"

She stared at me sadly. Sometimes I liked for a woman to look at me that way because I had a tendency toward self-pity. Sometimes I hated it because it meant they knew a broken toy wasn't going to be fun for long. This was the latter. I put on my shoes and my jacket. I gathered up the pages and stuck them in my jacket pocket. I wondered if I should kiss her goodbye or if I'd already blown the chance for that. I stood near her desk and she stood near her bed and we both stood like that for at least fifty-seven seconds too long.

I started for the door and she headed me off. She put her arms around me and I fell into them and she held me and shhhhed me again even though I wasn't making a sound. I knew then that I could love her. I might never be able to make her happy, but I knew I could love her.

She whispered in my ear, "Find Kathy Lark."

"I don't know where to start."

"That's easy. You lived down the street from her."

"I was ten. Her family moved away a long time ago."

"Start with your mother. Ask her what she remembers."

The drive back from Jersey was a blur of traffic, potholes, romantic meanderings, and prodded memories. The pages to the second act of the script were heavy in my pocket, but at least I had them. I hoped the other me had emailed them to Monty. I checked my phone. No messages from him. There was one from Celeste Campion, thanking me again for taking time out of my "busy schedule" to stop in and talk with her cinema appreciation club. She and the other members had found my "keynote speech" and "honest and informative Q & A" to be "inspiring, encouraging, and altogether dynamic." She invited me to stop in again anytime I wanted.

I hoped the other me had done a good job on the screenplay. I hoped the other me was the same other me and not some new other me who couldn't write worth a shit. I scrambled through Manhattan and got to the Midtown Tunnel and thought of the East River pouring in and washing me away. I thought of taking Eva on a Mediterranean cruise. I imagined her laid out on a beach in Greece with five-thousand-year-old ruins in the backdrop. Truck horns and sirens shattered what little concentration I had left.

I tried to focus on Kathy. You would've thought it would be easy, seeing how she'd been on my mind for almost thirty years, but it was difficult. She existed like some childhood story I'd heard over and over until it was a part of me but that I couldn't quite fully remember. I couldn't fully picture her face. I didn't know the sound of her voice. I couldn't remember anything we'd ever talked about or done together, except walking home from school together, silently, side by side.

I still didn't know why it was important for me to find her. It shouldn't have affected me any differently than it had every other kid in our class or in our neighborhood. There were more than enough other regrets, fears, and frustrations to haunt and harass a guy like me. I didn't need to worry about something from so long ago that just wasn't going to change my life for better or worse no matter what the answer turned out to be.

I jockeyed my way along the Long Island Expressway, spinning the dial on my brother's radio. Everything sounded wrong, out of tune, screeching, whining, warbling, squawking. I shut it off and hummed another polka.

When I got to the Robert Moses-Sagtikos Parkway exit I almost swung off. It was the way to Pilgrim State. I wondered what the new shrink would think about some of the events and experiences I'd been through since they'd cut me loose the last time. I wondered if I should tell her, "Yes, I loved Kathy. Yes, she's the only girl I've ever loved. No, I can't remember her much, hardly at all. Did you know your orderlies are selling spleens on the black market? What's your kickback on the ashtrays?"

I passed the exit. Just thinking about the ward was probably a good sign. Maybe. I couldn't be sure. I checked my eyes in the rearview. They looked the way they always did. A little puzzled, a little cruel, full of useless want. I eased down on the gas pedal. I sped along. I kicked it higher. I started burning past the other cars on the road. I wanted to get home. I hummed the "Village Inn Polka" louder.

I pulled into our neighborhood and drove slowly past Kathy Lark's house. The house that Kathy used to live in. Her parents and siblings had moved out less than a year after she went missing. At the time I remember my mother saying how odd it was that they'd leave so soon after Kathy had vanished. I agreed with her. I pictured Kathy turning up again, trying the front door, finding it locked, with another family living there. I imagined her anger and terror at that. I knew that if I ever disappeared and somehow found my way home again, I'd want to see my ma there to welcome me back.

Now I was surprised they had lasted almost a full year. Every second in that place must've reminded them that she wasn't there. That she had vanished. That she was most probably dead. That she had most probably died a heinous death. That there were men who prowled suburban streets intent on rape and torture. That such a man had probably stood in their yard, watching the lights go out in the windows. That he might have even been inside. That he had touched their belongings as well as their daughter. That he might still be revisiting them, carrying a watch bob made of Kathy's hair, cufflinks made of her teeth.

Christ, a year of that. How had they made it that long?

I slowed in front of the house. I had no idea who lived there now or how many families had been in and out of the place in the last three decades. Maybe only one, maybe dozens. It looked a lot like the way I remembered it back then, though I acknowledged that I hardly remembered the place at all.

I'd been told the cops had done a thorough search, but what might someone find if they tore up the concrete in the driveway, in the garage, in the foundation? If they dug ten feet down beneath the oaks, fifteen, twenty feet. If I went back there with a shovel, how many bones might I find?

The Memento Thief. Was this what he stole? The wrist bones of little girls?

I sat there in my dead brother's car, waiting for a dead little girl to come home again so I could move on and maybe finish act three to a script I couldn't read and that would never be made. The ludicrousness of the situation was not lost on me. Or on Tony Todesco. Or on Gideon. Or, looking in the rearview, on the other me, if it was him looking at me, and not just me. I couldn't tell who I was anymore.

"My name is Tommy Pic," I said. "Names have power. This one is mine. I'm Tommy Pic."

I looked in the rearview and said, "Who the fuck are you?"

The rearview looked at me and said, "Who the fuck are you?"

I drove up the street and parked in front of my mother's house. It hadn't changed much either. I'd spent over fifteen years in L.A. but when I'd gotten back again this place was just the same, as if I'd been the one who'd gone missing. As if I'd come crawling out of my grave. And my mother, of course, had been there to welcome me back.

My ma, my poor ma, never a minute's rest her whole life, what with me, Bobby, Deb, and Lawrence Welk always around.

I pulled into the driveway and sat there, wondering if she ever visited my old man's grave. We'd never been there as kids, not at Easter or Christmas or his birthday. I couldn't see her going alone, but that didn't mean it didn't happen. I tried to picture her standing there at his headstone, praying, meditating, weeping. My imagination failed me.

I climbed out of the car and walked into the house. Deb met me at the door. I had time enough to tighten up. She hit me low and hard like usual, but instead of sending me over the railing she just got me in a bear hug and hefted me off the floor. She spun me around twice, grunted a few words I couldn't understand, and a couple that I could.

She said, "Smell witchy."

At least that's what I thought she said. She put me down and stroked my hair twice like she was petting a dog.

A bus pulled up on the street and tooted its horn once. Deb grabbed a book bag off the kitchen table and said, "Bye Ma, bye Ta." She rushed out the door and onto the bus, and once she got to her seat she waved to me and I waved back until she was out of sight.

My ma was in the kitchen. She was cooking, of course, making meatballs while a big pot of pasta sputtered on the stove. It was 9:30 in the morning. My old man had been trim and muscular until the cancer had gotten him. I didn't know how he avoided being fat with all this food always around.

I took my seat and my mother asked, "Hey, where've you been?"

"Hoboken."

"Good god, why?"

"A friend had a party."

"Oh, that's nice. Did you have fun?"

It was a loaded question. My mother had visited me in a lot of wards over the years. She knew the word "fun" had a lot of meanings for a fuck-up like me. It could mean a laugh riot or a weekend in the drunk tank. It could mean did I get laid or did I manage to keep from breaking into a liquor store or terrifying an immigrant family on the subway. Did I have fun?

"Sure," I said. "Ma, tell me about Kathy."

For a minute nothing happened. She just kept kneading the ground beef and packing it into tight balls, which she set aside in a frying pan that was spitting oil. Then she went to stirring her pots. She washed her hands in the sink, and then washed them again, and then washed them again.

I was afraid she was going to wash her hands bloody. I said, "Ma?"

She rinsed her hands and dried them on a clean dish towel, facing away from me and looking out the kitchen window at the patio, where my father used to sit out on the Adirondack furniture, drink beer, and read the paper. Bobby used to do the same thing, a few years later, after Dad was gone. I wondered if she expected me to carry on the tradition. It had something to do with being the man of the house. Except I wasn't the man of the house. I was just the guy hiding in the basement.

Then my mother's shoulders drooped as if I'd just climbed up onto her back. She took a deep breath that sucked all the air out of the room. She let it out slowly in a thousand-year-old sigh. She turned and her face was an etched illustration of sorrow and impatience.

"Why do you want to bring all of that up again?"

I played it straight. It was something I rarely did with my mother. Or anyone. "I'm not bringing it up. It's just coming up on its own. It's always there. I can't get past it. I... I just think..."

"You think if you could find her your own life would change? That everything would go right for you? That you could write again and become successful once more?"

"I don't know," I admitted. "Maybe."

She came over and pressed her hands to the sides of my face and held me like that while I stared wide-eyed. Her hands were chilled from the cold water. They still smelled faintly of sauce, meat, grease, and the other things that made her smell like my mother. I tried to read her expression and couldn't do it.

"There's nothing for you to do, Tommy," she told me. "Kathy's been gone more than twenty-five years. You know that."

"I know that."

"The police combed the entire area. They asked a hundred people a thousand questions. We all looked. There were search parties all over the area."

"I know—"

"Every park, every grassy area along Southern State and Sagtikos Parkway, every school yard for miles around. The police did, whatever they call it, rousted dozens, hundreds of suspects. Perverts who'd been in prison for child abuse. Bad people."

She let go of my face as if my cheeks had singed her palms. She backed away until she was leaning against the counter. The sauce was boiling over. She didn't care. I'd never seen my mother not care about sauce before. I got up and lowered the flame on the stove. I looked at all the food. There was enough for a family of five, except we weren't five anymore, but Ma had never learned to cook for any less than that. It was a waste. It had always been a waste. But it showed that she, too, was thick with ghosts.

"What about her dad?" I asked.

"What about him?"

"I never liked him."

She scoffed. "That's because you were a spoiled brat and he used to send you home. Otherwise you would have stayed there all day and night. He'd tell you to leave so Kathy could do homework and you'd scream and start crying. That was my fault. After your father died I let you do almost anything you wanted. If I didn't, you'd throw a tantrum. You were sensitive. You wailed. You had nightmares where you thought you were down in the coffin with him. You were... uncontrollable."

"I was?"

"Kathy's father would call here and I'd walk up the block and grab you and have to practically drag you home. And it was difficult enough raising your sister and your brother. Bobby was always in all kinds of minor trouble. Out with the worst kind of girls. Couldn't hold a job, always fighting with his bosses. He was uncontrollable too, in his way."

"I recall you fighting with him."

He had lived in the basement back then. His first marriage was over by the time he was twenty. His two kids taken from him, and he never cared, never saw them, never paid child support.

"I fought with everyone," she said.

And my ma, my poor ma, who I'd never seen cry, not even when my dad had died, not all the times I was drunk and crazy and laid out strapped down to the mental ward beds, my ma never frazzled at all, handling it all because she was so strong, iron-willed, always taking care of whatever needed taking care of.

"But what about Kathy?" I persisted. "What do you remember?"

"What are you asking, Tommy? What do you want to know?"

"I'm not sure."

"Yes you are. Do you want me to tell you? Do I need to say it?"

"Tell me what? Say what?"

My ma, now breaking down into sobs, and she reached for me, the planes and angles of her face falling in on themselves, the meat burning in the pan, the grease spattering across the backs of my arms as she pressed me toward the flames and whimpered, "You were with her when she disappeared."

It wasn't easy breaking her grip. She was short, stout, and muscular. She'd spent her life working and slaving and I was a wimp who typed. It wasn't easy pretending I hadn't been burned. It wasn't easy hearing words I didn't believe but knew must be true because my own mother was saying them.

"No, I wasn't," I said.

The emotional weight dropped from her frame. She relaxed and her legs quivered. I took her and led her to a chair. She sat as if she had never sat before and was forcing her body to bend in ways it wasn't made to move.

I sat beside her, our knees touching. She was sixty-eight and now I saw every worry and stress line and wrinkle I'd ever carved into her flesh. It was like looking at my initials knifed into tree bark a thousand times over.

Her few tears ran down the gutters and valleys of her face and dried long before they got to her chin.

"You were. But you could never tell anyone anything about what happened."

"But—"

"The police brought in child psychologists."

"I was ten," I said, more forcefully than I'd intended. "I wasn't a child."

"A ten-year-old is a child. But nobody could ever get you to say what happened. You either repressed it all or you really didn't know much. Or you were traumatized by the incident. In the end, the FBI decided she was picked up in a car and abducted and you ran off."

I couldn't stay in my chair. I got to my feet and looked at the basement door and the front door and every window as if they offered escape. "If that were true, I would have said so."

"Unless you couldn't."

"Unless I couldn't? Why wouldn't I?"

"For some reason."

"What reason?"

She stared at me and her eyes were filled with terror and pain for me. "I don't know, Tommy."

But of course she knew. She was thinking the worst. I had gotten my imagination from somewhere. She had plenty of it, slopping bucketfuls, like most mothers. She had pictured me sodomized and abused and with a switchblade laid across my testicles and some hulking monstrosity hissing, *Say a word about this and I'll cut your little pecker off and stuff it down your throat.* She probably still did.

My tether might have snapped. I might have complexes and issues and lapses in judgment and rationale and reason. I might have crazy thoughts. I might be crazy. I might be possessed. I might be stuffed full of demonic familiars, spirits, and dragons. I might have an interior life more real and important to me than anything that happened to me in the normal light of day.

But was it possible that I could've seen Kathy being kidnapped or killed and not remember it?

"You're thinking I was sexually abused," I said.

"Oh good Christ! Don't say it!" She actually turned away from me, clamped her eyes shut, and started to put her hands over her ears.

I gripped her gently by the wrist and spun her back to face me. "Don't say it? Didn't the police give me a physical? Didn't you take me to a doctor?"

"Of course not!"

"Of course not?"

"They didn't do things like that back then," she said doggedly. "They didn't check for things... like that."

"They didn't? Why the hell not?"

"Not with boys, Tommy!"

"But what about forensic evidence?" I asked.

"They didn't do forensic evidence twenty-seven years ago!"

"Of course they did, Ma!"

At least I thought they did. But maybe I was wrong. And my ma, my poor ma, she was adamant, her jaw muscles tight and bulging beneath her ears, her gaze angled at the ceiling as she tried to push her mind somewhere else. My mother, I realized, had issues, complexes, and lapses in good judgment too.

"Besides," she said, "what good would that have done? To know that. You couldn't remember anything. It was better to leave you alone."

She had been so sure that I'd been tortured and raped and would have the stigma of sexual abuse heaped upon me all my life that she'd decided being uncertain forever was better. And all my life I'd proved to her that her suspicions were accurate, just because I was sensitive. Just because I was an asshole.

I became keenly aware of the pages in my pocket. Maybe *What Makes You Die* was my memoir. Maybe it wasn't a movie at all.

I shook my head. "This is ridiculous."

"I told you not to bring it up."

"You were right, Ma. You're always right."

I turned away. I felt caged in. I wanted out. I didn't know where out might be. Maybe Manhattan. Maybe Hoboken. Maybe Pilgrim. Maybe I needed to go sit in Celeste Campion's garage beneath the blazing eyes of Orson Welles and Ed Wood. I went to the front window. I craned my neck but I couldn't make out Kathy's house from here.

My mother's voice was so weary and distant that I thought maybe she'd left the room. "I'm sorry I couldn't help you."

I turned and was surprised to see her still at the kitchen

table. "You have. You told me the truth about Kathy."

"No, I'm sorry I've never been able to help you. Not with anything that mattered. That really mattered."

"Don't start that, Ma. Don't blame yourself."

"I don't. It's a simple and honest admission. I wanted to help you, but I couldn't."

"It's different now," I told her.

"What's different?"

"I am."

She sighed again. There was something in it that was almost a chuckle, almost a pained sob. "You say that, but —"

"I know, I've said it before."

She patted my face. She did it the way my grandmother did it. It was the You're a good boy pat. I didn't want to hear it. "You're —"

"What happened to Kathy's family? Where did they go?"

"You still think it matters?"

"Probably not, but I wonder."

She thought about it. "I heard Phoenix, but after all these years, who knows?"

I nodded. I sat and thought about it all and came to no conclusions. In about fifteen minutes, my mother put a plate of antipasto, meatballs, pasta and sauce in front of me. It was ten in the morning, but I ate because I was famished and because it made her happy. I hadn't had anything since Darla had fed me one of her bacony-cheese hors d'oeuvres. I finished everything my ma put in front of me.

I'd been with Kathy, there, at the end, whatever that ending had been.

By early afternoon I'd left Eva two boyishly charming messages on her voicemail. When I wasn't thinking about Kathy being murdered or my ten-year-old self being sodomized I was full of romantic sentiment. I tried hard not to picture Pye the pug playing back my messages and telling her, "What a goofy bastard."

Then I called Monty and left a message saying I'd finished act two, and asked if he had received it. He called back five minutes later, sounding put out.

"Why the hell are you asking me if I've received my email? Of course I did. Who doesn't get their email? I printed the file out and read it on the crapper this morning."

"You always know the right thing to say, Monty."

"It's solid. It's even stronger than the first act. We've got something here, Tommy. Like I told you the other day, it's special. It's different. It's sellable."

"That would make it different, all right," I said.

"You're doing things here you haven't done in a long time. I've already got a list of B-listers we can send it to. A couple of A-listers too, but don't get too delirious."

I said nothing. I wasn't going to get delirious.

When I didn't respond excitedly he got a little miffed. His voice hardened. "We're going to get offers. I'm glad you're staying off the hooch. Don't go off the wagon. You're still writing, aren't you? Will you have more of this done by Monday morning?"

"Maybe."

"Good. The more you finish, so long as it's of this quality, the better I'll be able to work the suits at the studios. And I appreciate you going out of your way for one of your stablemates."

"My... stablemate?"

"The angry clown role for Bango," Monty said. "That was really thoughtful of you. He'll nail it."

"Right. Sure. No trouble at all. We stablemates need to look after one another."

"Did you read my suggestions for the first act?"

"I did."

"And?"

"I thought they were very insightful."

"You prick. That's the kind of shit you tell an editor when you're not going to make any revisions."

"I'll take another pass, Monty, don't worry. I'll redraft."

The other me would either accept Monty's comments or not. It wasn't up to me.

"Good, because I've got more for the second act. I'm sending them on to you right now. Did you get my email?"

He was being a sarcastic son of a bitch but I knew that he actually had a reason, or thought he had a reason, this time. He was nervous. We were on the edge of perhaps doing something right again. Monty Stobbs had never been anxious about taking a meeting, crashing a party, icing out the competition, mouthing off to the suits. He must have actually had big hopes for *What Makes You Die*.

I checked. "I got your email, Monty."

"Wonderful. Keep working. Push yourself. Don't break down, don't ease up, don't go off the deep end, just work. Monday's the first day of the rest of your life."

"What about today?" I asked, and I wasn't even kidding.

He hung up.

His email read: NICE REASONING RE: GIRL BOX BOWL. THE MEMENTO THIEF IS FATHER? BROTHER? SISTER? A'S RESPONSE TO B'S DECLARATION IS BRUTAL BUT IN A FUN WAY. YOU WERE RIGHT TO KILL OFF GUY WITH THE SHOVEL. GOOD MOVE. WHERE IS FOOL'S CAP? WHERE IS FOOL'S GIRL'S CAP? THE MEMENTO THIEF'S EQUATION FOR HAPPINESS IS HILARIOUS. IS LEG IN CLOSET THE SAME LEG AS LEG IN THE BATHTUB? KID KNOWS KARATE?

They weren't quite as cryptic as before. I was starting to get a handle on the story, even if I couldn't read it. I could feel it. The other me had a lot of the same problems as I did, and he was trying to work them out with a lot of my own themes. So long as Monty thought it would sell we were working in the right direction.

I went to the bathroom mirror and gazed into my eyes. I wanted to high-five the bastard in there. I wanted to tell him, Don't blow your cool, you're doing well, hold on for just a little while longer. Two days. We can handle that, can't we? Just another two days?

He looked back at me and I knew what he was thinking.

Hell no.

Mirrors had power, too. I remembered what I'd read in one of the books in Weird Sisters. A scrying mirror could show you what you needed to know, what you needed to see. I stared and stared. I stared until I felt like I was going blind. I heard Deb come home and trundle across the living room and turn on Lawrence. I kept staring. I looked more deeply into the scrying mirror, praying to whatever dark gods and goddesses might take pity on me. It didn't do anything. It didn't cloud and show me new scenes I wanted to see, of distant places, of the past or the future. It offered no answers. It was just a mirror and showed me my own angry face. I knew that real magic worked differently from how people who used rooster hearts and goofer dust and peppers and dried mouse entrails thought it worked.

The other me had nothing more to say. I kept staring.

And I saw.

I saw the reflection of my face, but there was something different this time.

I saw the coven tree again. And the pyre. And the sacrifice that I had stopped. I watched witches dancing around someone tied to the tree. The women were naked. Their faces were white; their eyes were black. I liked dead chicks. The sacrifice was a struggling man. He snarled and snapped his teeth. He was drunk and he was ignorant. I thought it was me but it was only someone who looked like me. I could feel memories beginning to shift, break away, and float to the surface. I continued staring.

More memories returned. They weren't revelations. They were just film clips, a few extra frames here and there. The director was one of those highly stylized pretentious jagoffs. I hated him immediately. I saw the back of a man's head, sitting at the wheel of a moving car. A flash of a face in the side-view mirror. A scrape on the bumper. A little cigarette smoke drifting from the open driver's window. Water dripping from the tailpipe. A stretch of lawn, treetops waving as the wind grew stronger. A speckle of rain striking a window, a car roof, a windshield, an empty curb. The man flicking out his cigarette and rolling up the window. His foot easing down on the brake, pulling the car over.

I can't hear the soundtrack, though. I don't know if it's low and ominous, full of spooky stingers, or just music on the radio, something bluesy maybe. The rumble of the muffler will offer a natural sense of foreboding. The rain can go either way. If it's chilly and the skies are darkening, it can be another sign of apprehension and misgiving. If it's like silver needles coming down, it can be sleek and urbane, foreshadowing an action scene. If someone drops to his knees and looks to the heavens' drops as he's washed in the storm, it can express a grand show of redemption.

Now we see kids on the sidewalk, running, laughing in the rain. A boy and a girl. The girl clearly more mature, the boy a jumble of silly angles. Elbows, a cockeyed smile, a goofy face. His coat is buttoned wrong, his hair a mess, his left shoe untied. You can tell he's fatherless because his father would never put up with this sort of thing. What father doesn't shout, "Go tie your shoe, will you? You look like a moron." The kid thinks of movies all day long, never focuses on school. He's clearly in the dumb kids' class. But there's something in his eyes, a hint of a former version of himself, that elicits the feeling that he might have been very different before. He might've been sharp, he might have been a regular kid. The girl is showing a great kindness just for spending even this small amount of time with him, on their walk home, in the rain.

I want to run the film again. I want to rewind. I want to shout up to the projector booth to roll it once more. You always miss important details the first time around. You always spot something in the background, just out of focus, that some sly director has left in so that on repeated viewings you say about the elitist fuck, "Well, well, look at that."

Okay, now we were getting somewhere. It was obvious to me what was going to happen, what it all meant. I groaned in the bathroom. The scrying mirror clouded with my breath. The pipes in the walls creaked and moaned with water as Debbie flushed upstairs. I shut my eyes. When I opened them again there was a Post-it note from Gideon stuck to the glass. It read: TO SEE MORE IS TO FIND OBLIVION. THIS IS WHAT MAKES YOU DIE. I pulled it off, crumpled it, and tossed it in the waste can. The film moved on.

But I knew what was coming next. I was familiar with this next part even if I hadn't remembered before. I recognized how it would unfold before it happened. It didn't scare me. It wasn't a horror story. It wasn't a thriller. Maybe it was a documentary or just a home movie.

"Ah, Ma," I said.

I hadn't forgotten because I'd been traumatized. I hadn't forgotten because I'd been sexually abused or seen horrors that had fractured my tiny sensitive mind. We might repress such one-of-a-kind scenarios, but we never really forgot them. They're forced back up in our dreams; they come out in the writing.

We don't remember the small repetitions that occur every day. We don't remember putting our shoes on, we forget our drives to work. We forget because we do it every day. We don't think about it, we don't grasp hold anymore. It flashes by, day in and out. I'd forgotten what I'd seen because it meant nothing to me.

The driver, pulling over to the curb, rolling the passenger side window down. Close-up on his chin—still unable to make out the face—turning to the kids rushing along getting wet. The girl smart enough to put the hood of her coat up, the boy just stumbling over cracks in the cement with his hair getting drenched. He really does look like a moronic ten-year-old. It'll be the last time he ever smiles quite so widely.

The driver turns down the radio. He says, "Hey, get in, I'll take you the rest of the way home." His voice is familiar. Of course it is. It was familiar then. It's familiar now. As he speaks, the scrying mirror clouds up from its depths, from the other side of the glass. I'm a little surprised to realize that I miss the sound of that voice.

The boy and the girl scramble into the back seat together. In another six or seven years they might lose their virginity to each other in this back seat. Maybe it's wishful thinking, maybe it's the truth. Or could have one day been the truth.

The girl says, "Thanks!"

The driver says, "That's okay!"

The boy says, "It's wet out there," showing his utter grasp of the obvious and the puerile.

The car proceeds along, block after block, for no more than a half a mile, but it feels longer with the rain coming down. The girl—let's call her by her name now, because it has to be done—Kathy says something about the bluesy music. She likes it. She knows it. Her father plays it.

The driver—the driver is my brother, Bobby—I can see the side of his face now, and he looks like me, the man in the mirror, or the other me, the man in the mirror. He looks like us. He grins. He says something about the band's better-known song. Does she know that one too? She does.

The boy—me—sitting in the back, adding nothing to the conversation, water running into my eyes, because I never did pull the hat out of my pocket although my mother made me take it. I'm looking around for an old flannel rag, several of which my brother keeps in the trunk but not in the back seat. I look around for a chamois cloth, several of which my brother keeps in the trunk, but none in the back seat. I unzip my jacket and wipe my wet face with the tails of my shirt.

We come to our house. Bobby pulls into the driveway. I squeak out, "Bye, Kathy!" She says, "See you tomorrow!"

I run into the house as the car moves down the street toward Kathy's house.

There was no reason to remember such a thing. It had happened many times before. The face of the driver was one I had known all my life.

The car was the car I had been driving for two years.

I shut my eyes. I pressed my forehead to the glass. I whispered her name. The other me whispered her name.

Lawrence Welk didn't whisper her name, but continued on with "The Champagne Polka."

When I opened my eyes I saw that Gideon had left another Post-it note.

WAS I RIGHT?

"No," I said.

I tore the note off the mirror, shredded it, and threw the pieces in the toilet. I flushed it away.

My brother had died in his own blood and shit from hep A, B, or C, on my mother's couch. I might die the same way. We hardly ever saw each other even while I lived at home. He was always busy with his wives and kids, all of them stuffed in the basement along with him while he drove his route and fucked housewives in the back of the bus.

He was in the basement before me. He stayed there when I went to L.A. When I got back he was dead and I took over in the basement. The scrying mirror had been full of his many faces long before it had been filled with mine.

I stopped staring. I checked my watch. I'd been looking in the mirror for almost eight hours. I moved away and almost fell over. My legs had gone to sleep. I rubbed them vehemently and rode out the vicious and painful pins and needles, my mouth clamped shut against my groans.

Twenty minutes later I went upstairs. My sister said, "Huh Ta."

"Hi Deb."

I sat at the kitchen table in my seat and watched my mother rushing around from pot to pan and back again. She was making a new meal. I'd eaten the pasta and meatballs for breakfast. I smelled chicken broiling in the pan. My stomach growled.

I didn't know how to word it. I didn't know how to say what I needed to say, so I just let it out.

"It was Bobby," I said.

"What's that?" my mother asked.

"It was Bobby," I repeated. "He took her, Ma. Kathy. That's what I saw the day she disappeared."

"Yes," my mother said. She was making more antipasto, potatoes, broccoli in vinegar and oil, and fried spinach patties. "He picked up the two of you and dropped you off here at home and then drove her up the street and let her out. You told us that. He told us that."

That stopped me. My legs still hurt. I kept rubbing them. I squinted at her. "I did? He did?"

"Of course. Why? Did you think your brother had something to do with her going missing?"

"I... but I... I didn't remember. I didn't remember him being there until just now."

She turned and stared at me. It was the look. Christ, I hated the look. She said, "You told us exactly what happened. He drove the two of you home often.

"But, wait... why didn't he drop her off first, and then come back home here with me?"

"He was always going out, you know that. He was always chasing girls. The police questioned him for hours. You really don't remember any of this?"

The look. Gideon turned around and crawled deeper into my bowels.

"No."

"He wasn't a suspect. Bobby had an alibi. He dropped her off and went over to some girl's house or another, picked her up, went out to a burger place, got drunk. I think it was... I think it was *that one* he was seeing." My mother's code for his first wife. "He was seen all over town."

"The trunk," I said. "The car trunk. He could've—"

"The police went over the car. And the basement. And his clothes. And your clothes too. And our garage. And all our property. And the neighbors. And the Lark home. They tore up Mrs. Lark's azaleas. The searched. They searched everywhere. And they questioned everyone who ever had any contact with that little girl. They were very thorough." She looked at me like she'd never seen me before. I felt puny. Gideon had been right. This was oblivion, digging up old graves. "Did you really suspect your own brother? After all this time? That's what went through your mind?"

"I thought I was remembering something new. Something I might have blocked."

My mother turned all the burners on the stove down. I was going to get her full attention again. I didn't want it. I'd made a mistake. I wanted to apologize to my brother's face. I wanted to smash the scrying mirror. I wanted to tell my ma, No, not the look, please not the look.

"It wasn't your fault. What happened to her wasn't your fault."

"I know that."

"But you don't really believe it. You never have. It's always been a sliver in your heart that you were somehow responsible."

"That's not true, Ma."

"It is true, Tommy," she said. She put her fists on the kitchen table and leaned down onto them. It was a pose that men made all the time, but I'd never seen a woman do, much less my ma. "It's always been true. That's why you've suffered so much. Why you've made yourself so miserable."

"I don't make myself miserable."

She turned back to the stove. The oil began to sizzle and pop again. I knew the other me wasn't going to finish act three unless something else happened. Some answer was found, some sacrifice was made, some memory unearthed. I wondered, Where is Fool's cap? Where is Fool's girl's cap? I wanted to know what the Memento Thief's equation for happiness might be.

I fled downstairs again. I said, "I'm sorry," aloud to the ghost of my brother, if he was anywhere nearby, and if he could hear me. It was all right that we didn't like each other, it was all right that I was afraid of becoming him. It wasn't fair that I had imagined him a murderer just because he was an ignorant prick. If he heard me, he didn't respond.

I got online and checked for Kathy's family in Arizona. I remembered her father's name was Cal. I didn't know if it was short for Caleb or Calvin or maybe Callum, but it should stand out. I found nothing. I suspected my mother had lied to me about hearing they'd moved to Phoenix. I did a search on her old address up the block and got nowhere. I wasn't a private eye and had no idea how to hunt somebody down.

I found the Suffolk County White Pages online and plugged in the name C. Lark.

And just like that, there it was.

Caleb Lark.

Caleb Lark, clinical psychotherapist. Therapist.

I knew what the jargon meant. You didn't need any kind of a degree to hang out a shingle calling yourself a therapist. Kathy's father probably saw clients in his den and did a lot of nodding and *I understand*ing. Maybe he helped people. Maybe he helped himself.

The street address surprised me. The Lark family hadn't moved far. They were twenty minutes away, two towns west of us.

I phoned and got a receptionist. I would've bet anything that I was talking to Kathy's mother. I wanted to shake something loose. I asked to see the "doctor." She didn't correct me, of course. She said he was booked up for the next three weeks. I said it was an emergency. She asked me if I was having suicidal thoughts. I said yes. She asked me my name and I answered, "Tony Todesco." She told me to come right over, they'd fit me in.

I thought that was nice. I appreciated her effort and felt guilty for lying. I wondered if my guilt would lead me to contemplate suicide, just so I wouldn't be a liar. Everything evened out somehow, eventually.

She gave me directions. I got into my dead brother's Impala and started it up. But I couldn't pull out of the driveway until I got out and checked the trunk.

Kathy wasn't there. The flannel rags and chamois clothes were.

I drove over to the Lark house. The place looked very much like the one they'd owned up the road from us. The mother's azalea bushes were in the same spot. There was a side door with a shingle hung out front. CALEB LARK, CLINICAL PSY-CHOTHERAPIST.

I spent a while looking around, as if Kathy might had been nearby, hiding, watching, for years, waiting to go back home again. I wanted to be the one who said it was all right. I turned and turned again, and again, facing in every direction, so that she might see me and know that someone had never forgotten her. That I was still waiting for her to return to me.

I walked up the little porch to Caleb Lark's side office. I knocked. I wondered if I would recognize him after all this time.

He answered the door with a disarming smile. He looked good. He was trim and carried himself with an athlete's coordination. He still had all his hair. There was less gray in it than in mine. He put his hand out and I took it and we shook. Some kind of current passed between us. Maybe it was just a small charge from stepping on the carpet. Maybe it was ball lightning forming in the sky above us. I waited for a burst of electrons to ignite between us and blow us apart. It didn't happen. We kept shaking. His grip was strong. Mine was weak.

It took a few seconds, but his smile eventually froze on his face. Recognition flooded his gaze. He was sharp and sensitive, maybe even as sensitive as me. His lips flattened into a bloodless line. His expression hardened.

He said, "Hello, Tommy, nice to see you again. It's been a while. Come in."

He dropped his hand and I dropped mine, and we faced each other until he gestured for me to enter. He moved out of my way and I stepped inside.

If he felt like I'd abused his trust, lying to him about my name, convincing him to see an emergency case of a potentially suicidal new client, he didn't say anything about it.

He extended his hand toward a nice leather recliner and said, "Have a seat." It was a little less obvious than having a couch in the office. I didn't sit. He took his chair behind his desk. There was a pen and a pad there but he didn't pick them up.

WHAT MAKES YOU DIE

I noticed there were no photos on his desk or walls, either. I was hoping he'd have one of Kathy, just so I could see her again. I was slightly offended and a little pissed that he didn't have a framed picture of her to glance at all the time. And where were his wife and other kids?

"You don't look well," he said.

"And you don't look surprised to see me," I said.

"I'm not. I always thought you'd seek us out eventually."

"Why?"

"To either tell us more about what happened that day or to ask us if we knew anything else about Kathy."

I hated how easily he took the role of doctor, expecting me to be the patient. He didn't have any initials after his name. He wasn't a psychiatrist or even a psychologist. It was all a ruse, just like with ten thousand other pricks who pretended to be able to help someone because they'd taken a Psych 101 course or read the latest bestselling self-help tract. I went to his bookcase and looked through the titles. I always did that. If he'd had his DVDs on display I'd be checking them out too.

His shelves were full of textbooks on relationships, child rearing, grief counseling, depression, how to diet your way to a healthy mind, why bad things happen to good people. *I'm Okay, You're a Schizoid Fuck*. I wondered if he would someday study the Memento Thief's Equation for Happiness.

Lark said, "I heard you'd moved to Hollywood and become quite successful, for a time."

"That's a minor barb couched in a distancing technique," I said. "To say you 'heard' it... as if you weren't interested but someone offered up the information anyway, maybe while you were only half-listening, perhaps at a cocktail party. Was that the case?"

"My son, Roger, mentioned it a number of years ago. But where's the perceived barb?"

"The addition of 'for a time.' Quantifying my success and connoting that it's already ended. In conversation with someone else it would just be an acknowledgment of fact. Saying it to me was clearly intended to make me bristle."

"And you did," Lark said.

"Of course." I stepped to his desk and stood before it, staring down at him. "So if my career is of no real interest to you, then let's not bother discussing it."

"All right, if that's your wish, Tommy."

"That's another disarming tactic, Mr. Lark. 'If that's your wish.' As if you're going out of your way to comply with my desires when it was you yourself who admitted you didn't give a damn about my accomplishments or lack thereof. And for the record, nobody over the age of ten makes a 'wish' anymore."

"You want to discuss Kathy's disappearance."

"I do."

"That's why you just mentioned 'the age of ten.' You're unconsciously focused."

"I'm consciously focused," I admitted. "But that's beside the point."

"Do you have something to tell me, Tommy?"

"No, Clinical Psychotherapist Cal Lark, I do not."

He tried to give me the look, but he was a complete amateur. He just sat there and frowned. I should've felt sympathy for him, having gone through losing his daughter, his life being wrecked, all the misery. But I hadn't liked him as a kid and I still didn't.

He said, "You're being very aggressive."

"I've dealt with a lot of shrinks. I know the ploys to get under someone's skin. To jangle the nerves. To dig for the truth, to accept a token position of power. You've been doing it since I walked in. Now, do you want to talk or do you want to keep playing these ludicrous analyst games with me?"

He sat a little farther back in his chair. "Let's talk."

"Good."

He didn't have to catalogue or organize his thoughts. It was all right there, on the tip of his tongue, as if he, like me, had been waiting decades to face each other again. "At the time you said you couldn't remember anything besides the fact that your brother Bob picked you and Kathy up while you were walking home from school."

"In the rain."

"Yes. Bob claimed to let you out at home and then dropped her off at our house moments later. Do you remember anything more than that?"

"No," I said. "I didn't even remember my brother picking us up at all until earlier today. It was something he did all the time. He cruised for chicks. He dated a lot of neighborhood girls. It didn't stand out in my mind all these years."

"Did anything?"

"Just the fact that I missed Kathy."

"Then you've got nothing to add. No new information to impart. No repressed memories have surfaced, no clues, nothing."

"Right," I said. "Nothing. I was hoping you might have something to tell me instead."

"Why?"

Why? I wanted to tell him, Because I'm sensitive. Because I was the goofy dumbass kid clowning with your daughter, who loved her in my own ten-year-old goofball way. She's alive within me from minute to minute more than she is in you, her own father. I see her on the streets. I see her in the river. I write scripts about her. The movie is always playing, and she and I are in the seventh row center eating candy together.

"Because more than twenty-five years have passed and I haven't seen you since I was ten. There could've been news of some sort."

"There hasn't been."

"Nothing?"

"No, nothing."

"There has to have been something!" I shouted. "Anything! A ransom note, her bones, a serial killer who listed her as a possible victim! Someone must've remembered something new.

You! Your wife! Your kids. Roger! Roger used to give me wedgies whenever he saw me, the little son of a bitch. Roger probably knows some evil shit!"

"There's nothing, Tom."

It was easy to hate Cal Lark, Clinical Psychotherapist because he had learned to live with his daughter having gone missing. He hadn't committed suicide. He hadn't gone to the madhouse. He hadn't blown all his fuses. He continued on. My heart slammed inside my chest. My pulse rate doubled and snapped in my wrists. My carotid felt like it might blow arterial spray across the ceiling any second.

"You need professional help, Tommy," he said.

"You can't help me," I said.

"We can talk, Tommy. We can always talk. I can accept you as a patient, if you'd like."

"You can't help me," I repeated. It was the truth.

I walked to the door and he clambered from behind his desk and came after me. It was a dramatic moment. I'd seen a lot of movies with similar scenes. Now there would be revealing dialogue. The killer would make his mistake. Cal Lark would give away some small clue that would betray him and indicate he'd murdered his own daughter. I took him by the shoulders and shook him. He was trim and strong but I could snap him into splinters if I wanted. I glared at him, searching his eyes. There was nothing. He said nothing. He revealed nothing.

I turned my back on him and left.

There was an answer. Kathy had either been kidnapped or murdered. She was either right at this moment living as some madman's wife, brainwashed with no knowledge of her past, or chained up in a shed, or buried under fifty tons of rock in a gravel pit or out in the middle of the pine barrens. There was an answer, but I was never going to learn it.

I had known that. I had known that since the day she'd vanished. I had lived with it as well as I could. Maybe not as well as her father had, but I did it whatever way I had to.

WHAT MAKES YOU DIE

She was the great love of my life, made even greater because she would always remain a myth and a mystery. I could love her perfectly in my small understanding of her. She would never grow old, never argue with me, never disappoint me, and best yet, I would never fail her.

On the way home I stopped off at a liquor store and got myself a bottle of scotch. I brought it home and drank while I got online and found the website for the Queensland Museum in Australia. I found the staff page and chose the kindest face I could. It was an older woman, Dr. Mavis Norell, the senior curator of geosciences and comparative zoology. She offered up a quaint and quirky grin. That was all I needed.

I drank the booze and went to the bathroom scrying mirror. I tore it off its hinges and brought it with me into my living room where my laptop was set up. I turned the mirror at an angle to face the computer screen. I shoved it closer until they touched. I had put all of myself into my writing. Whatever was left over was in the glass.

I wrote a letter to Dr. Mavis Norell explaining that I was currently possessed by a member of the monitor lizard group, *Varanidae*, named Gideon, originally from the island of Gili Dasami before it was killed by an early hominid during the Pleistocene Age, quite possibly an ancestor of mine, which would explain our connection. His fossil was currently on display at the museum. I was through with the fucker and wanted him to get out of my guts. I couldn't carve him out so I was giving him to her as a gift. Along for the ride would be my friend Tony Todesco, who'd died delivering newspapers and had never lived long enough to grow into an adult. He'd never been out of the US and I thought he would enjoy a visit to beautiful Australia. They lived inside of me and I lived inside my writing, and in composing a missive to her I was handing them over the way I handed over everything that mattered to, loved, soothed, afflicted or tormented me. The gutted Portuguese kids might be along for the ride. My dead brother Bobby might show up too. So too my father and possibly the baby from the bin, who might or might not be real. I made sure that Dr. Mavis Norell realized she didn't have to do anything to receive these ghosts and I would have no further contact with her so she didn't need to alert authorities here or abroad. If paranormal activity did become aroused at the museum she should contact the Ghost Chasers International branch. I gave her all the contact information. I wished her well and in valediction, signed my email, *Please receive, Madam, my sincerest salutations.*

Like Eva had said: It's not always the gift that matters. It's the spirit in which it is given. The offering itself has virtue and influence. I punched the send button. My ghosts were on their way.

I spent all of Sunday in bed. Eva hadn't called back. I'd botched it with her. Maybe Pyewacket had advised her not to date me anymore. Maybe Darla blamed me for ruining the party for not letting the witches and the emo-leather-deathers sacrifice the redhead. Maybe I'd just spooked her. I figured it would be bad form to walk into Weird Sisters and ask for a love potion and then try to sprinkle it onto her bagels.

I hung the mirror back up in the bathroom. I stared in it only as long as it took me to wash my face and brush my teeth. If the other me was in there, he wasn't talking anyway. I finished the bottle of scotch and got into a nice relaxed state and watched a lot of cable TV. I caught a couple of movies written by friends of mine. I glared at flicks by some of Monty's other clients, my stablemates. I slept and didn't dream.

Kathy was one ghost I could never rid myself of because, despite her having the most impact on me, I really never had her at all.

I stewed as I watched the films. I sneered and I laughed. I drank and buzzed and felt warmth and got the chills. I swathed myself in blankets. I checked my phone like a high school kid, counting the minutes, waiting for Eva, craving attention. I took the pages of act one and act two and carried the weight of them both. I lay there glaring at the flicks, listening to the voices of friends and enemies on the commentaries, as if they were speaking directly to me. I lay there with the unfinished script of *What Makes You Die* on my chest. I pulled up my shirt, fingered the hara-kiri scar on my belly, and tried not to miss Gideon too much.

The day crawled. I hadn't been this alone in, well, possibly my whole life. The scotch didn't kill the feeling, it just enhanced it. In the bin there at least would've been some action. A little screaming, howling, weeping, declarations of love and hate, platitudes, the stink of feces being used to scrawl on the walls, the death matches in the day room.

The need to talk to Eva was overwhelming. The lack of a call back was like being forced to swallow ten thousand needles. There was no way to forget. There was no way not to realize, second by second, that the chance for love was already gone.

Monty called twice more, asking for progress reports on the third act. I told him it was coming along. He had even more meetings lined up. I figured if even a third of what he was claiming was true, I might be on the verge of a real second chance.

I slept hard without dreams. I woke at dawn moderately hungover. I downed aspirin and drank three glasses of water. I showered, shaved, and put on my best suit with a white shirt and power tie. I wanted to make an impression on the studio reps. I wasn't sure why. I didn't have a love of writing anymore, as proven by the fact that I hadn't done any in ages. My passion had been given, or stolen, by the other me. I wondered if he'd been sent to the Queensland Museum along with all the others in my email.

Even if I could garner some success again in Hollywood, there was always a chance it would be ripped out from under me again. A better than even chance. Almost everybody, no matter how far up they got on the ladder, wound up dropping to the bottom before it was all over. What was the point of even trying again? If I burned out a second time, in a year or five from now, making D-grade Zypho movies or flicks just like them, I was fairly certain it would land me in the bin forever.

I stood at the foot of the driveway holding a briefcase. I hadn't even known I owned a briefcase, but here it was. I had no idea what was inside it. I was about to hit the snaps when the limo cruised up. The driver climbed out, tipped his cap at me, opened the rear door for me, and said, "Good morning, sir."

"Hello."

"Plenty of time to catch your flight if you'd like to stop somewhere for breakfast first."

"No, thanks, I'm fine."

I got in back and he shut the door and facing directly opposite me on the wide leather seat was Bango, the angry clown, my stablemate, dressed in a full harlequin outfit. He squeezed his bitter horns at me.

"You coming to the meetings, Bango?"

He tooted and aroogaed me.

"Jesus Christ, man, can't you break character when it's just the two of us in the back of a fucking limo headed for Kennedy?"

He whaa-waaed and weep-wahhed me.

Maybe Bango was dead and I had a new phantom. Maybe he was just a mental representation of my fears and self-hatred and complete belief that I was a fool. Or maybe he was just a method actor keeping to his part and Monty really did have him flying to the West Coast with us to stir some action at the studios, or to do parties for the kids of the rich and famous.

We cruised west on the Southern State Parkway, fighting morning traffic. The driver was good. He didn't have a lot of room to move as he jockeyed lane to lane, but he did it smoothly and easily.

I eyed the bar. It was 6:30 in the morning. Bango saw me looking and blatted at me. He poured two big glasses of Jack Daniels on ice and tried to force one on me.

"Too early," I said, even though I wanted it.

He weep-wahhed at me a half dozen times, jamming the drink at my hand.

"No, Bango."

He put down the drinks and took off his shoe and tried hitting me in the head with it. I gave him a short jab to the chin and he fell back and settled down and sipped his drink, leering.

Fifteen minutes from Kennedy my phone rang.

It was Eva.

She said, "Sorry to call so early, I hope I didn't wake you."

"No, I'm up."

"I apologize for not getting back to you but there's been trouble at the store and even more at home. The store was robbed."

"If you can't trust witches—"

Bango awoogaed and sipped his drink.

"If someone's going to use our ritual elements for black magic, I suppose they think they might as well steal them. Evil begets evil. And then there was even more trouble at home. Darla had a big breakup with her boyfriend. They argued, he got physical, we had to call the cops, it got ugly. And after all that, she took him back as soon as it was time to press charges."

"Which one was her boyfriend?"

"I don't know if you met him or not. A big lug, always talking about guns, the war, who we should drop atomic bombs on."

"Evil begets evil," I said.

"Yes." A few seconds went by. "I left you two messages last night. I thought you would've called back. Or were you busy with your screenplay?"

I checked the phone and sure enough, there were two messages from her. I'd looked twenty times and had never seen them. Maybe I hadn't wanted to see them, or was too drunk to see them, or the other me was too busy to see them. "Sorry, I had it turned off. I was working. I'm sorry we didn't get a chance to talk."

"We can talk now. I'm off today. You can come over if you like. Darla and her boyfriend went to the Poconos to make up for their squabble. And the night he spent in a jail cell."

Bango pushed the Jack Daniels at me again. I looked into his painted face, his red nose, and figured he'd never get through security and he'd spend hours with Homeland Security getting his giant shoes x-rayed and his prostate probed. I pushed the drink off and slid over to the far corner of the seat.

"What does your armband tattoo say?" I asked her.

"And all my days are trances, and all my nightly dreams, are where thy gray eye glances, and where thy footstep gleams, in what ethereal dances, by what eternal streams."

"I like it," I said. "Poe. *To One in Paradise.*"

"That's right." She sounded impressed that I would know. "You like what it says?"

"I like what it says and I like that you have a tattoo. And I like where it is on you."

"Why?"

"I find it very sexy," I admitted. "An armband. Sort of Grecian. Warrior woman. I don't know, but I dig it."

"I know you do. You paid special attention to it. I like that you did that."

"I'm glad." I was starting to feel lonely for her again. "Is that what we're doing, enjoying an ethereal dance?"

"We did more than that, Tommy."

There was roadwork ahead. The right lane was closed and traffic was piling in around us and the limo driver was scooting and edging and gunning it when he could. Car horns blared. Whenever they did, Bango added to the noise with a little wahh-blaatt or woog-woog.

"Where are you?" she asked.

"Headed to the airport with an angry clown to meet my agent and fly to Los Angeles to take some meetings."

"Is this about the script that you printed out on my printer?"

"Yes."

"What Makes You Die."

"Yes."

"It's a terrific read, Tommy. I'm sure it would make a fine film. A successful one. I hope the powers that be do right by you."

"Thanks, I appreciate it."

WHAT MAKES YOU DIE

For two people who had only spent a few hours together total, we seemed to have a long and strange history. There were topics of all sorts to bring up, questions I should ask, comments I should make. We'd made love and I hadn't sent flowers. I was annoyed at myself for that. I'd taken her for granted already. My ex-wife would undoubtedly understand. I should be whispering sweet nothings, or sweeter somethings, or telling her how much I enjoyed watching her sleep, and nuzzling with her, and being a part of her. I could write a twenty-page scene about her ponytail bobbing.

"Did you ask your mother about Kathy?" Eva asked.

"I did."

"What did you learn, Tommy?"

I told her. About what I had remembered, and what my ma had said, and what Cal Lark, Clinical Psychotherapist had added, and how none of it meant anything in the long or short run because Kathy was still missing and would always be missing. I had lived with it for more than twenty-five years, but I hadn't lived with it well. I was going to have to learn.

Bango was giving the finger to some kids in the back seat of an SUV driving in the lane next to us. The kids were flipping him the bird right back.

"When will you be back?" Eva asked.

"I don't know. Monty wasn't very detailed with his itinerary. I'm betting at least half of what he said was bullshit. If we wind up having two meetings with some guys fresh out of the mailroom I'll count myself lucky. We'll probably be back in a couple days."

"Call me and let me know how things turn out."

"Okay."

"And I'll see you when you get back."

"Yes, you will," I said.

Bango and I met up with Monty at the check-in. Apparently Bango was real and not a psychological manifestation representing my childhood or my cynicism or some other

145

shit. He also proved that airport security was still horribly lax. Bango took off his big shoes, his horns, his red nose, his hat with bells on it, and his wig, and stuffed them in the tray. He walked through the metal detector with no problem. The lady checking the tray contents spotted nothing out of the normal. At the end of the conveyor Bango took out his stuff and put it all back on. Monty and I walked along with him and we marched down to our gate.

Monty wanted to talk about the script and give me a breakdown on exactly how he planned to deal with the execs. I listened without responding until we boarded. Then I told him, "Sounds great, Monty, you're going to be back on top soon." It might not be a lie.

He asked for the third act. I handed him my briefcase. I still didn't know what was in it. He popped the snaps and went through it. He sounded happy.

I took the window seat, Bango sat in the middle, and Monty took the aisle. Bango never said a word but kept playing his horns until we were over Pittsburgh. Then a whole group of folks in our general area bitched him out to the stewardess and she confiscated his horns. Without them he just sat there miming that he was crying. I shut my eyes and slept the rest of the way.

We landed at LAX and the same kind of nervous imperative tension filled me that had the first time I'd landed in Los Angeles when I was nineteen. The world was charged with blazing possibilities.

Monty said the third act was terrific. He sounded slightly awestruck. I should have been proud but I was a little nervous about it. He had an itinerary. I'd never known him to follow a schedule before. He'd rented another limo to pick us up from the airport. We were meeting folks at major studio offices, as well as a couple of indie producers. Names have power. I didn't recognize anybody he mentioned. I told him it all sounded good to me. Bango confirmed by weep-wahhing.

As we waited at the luggage carousel Monty asked, "Are you all right, Tommy?"

"Yes."

"You've hardly said a word the whole trip."

"So what? Bango hasn't said anything at all."

"No, but he's been miming a lot. He's been doing charades nonstop and acting shit out. He's driving me nuts. He won't put his hands down and shut up."

"Don't give him his horns back yet."

"Fuck no."

We found our limo driver holding a sign with STOBBS printed on it. We got in back and started in on the L.A. freeways. First stop was going to be a Kinko's. Monty wanted to make twenty copies of the completed script of *What Makes You Die*.

I let the day wash over me as if I were lying in the ocean letting the waves and current sway me about. I wouldn't resist or fight. I wouldn't demand or deny or grieve. I thought of my ex, and Eva, and Kathy, and Celeste Campion, and Dr. Mavis Norell. I thought of my ma, my poor ma, and Deb, and Aunt Carmela, and Grandma, and my cousins Jane and Caroline, and all their kids stampeding through the house, including the baby in the bin. I didn't need them to save me. I didn't even need to save myself. Because I wasn't dying or losing my mind. I was just thrashing around across the bottom of my life like damn near everybody.

We stopped for lunch at the Pacific Dining Car. I said, "Won't we be having lunch with any of the execs?"

"Maybe," Monty said, "but we can't go into any of these meetings on an empty stomach. Have a high-protein meal now, then eat salads if we go out again."

Bango tried ordering off the menu by playing charades but Monty told the waitress, "Jesus Christ, just bring him a steak, medium-well."

I ordered the same. I drank only fruit juice. I felt clear-headed for the first time in forever. I just wanted Monty to stop chattering at me, but he couldn't. The other me had apparently finished the third act and revisions sometime during my funk yesterday. Monty kept asking me who I saw in certain roles. I had no real ideas but Bango apparently did. He mimicked some big name actors and the tourists in the restaurant thought he was part of a floor show. He chased after some old man and threatened to throw the guy's lunch out the window, but Monty jumped up to stop the angry clown in time. Bango took a flamboyant bow and aroogaed his thanks as the other diners applauded him.

Back in the limo we shot off toward our first meeting. Monty had some complicated game plan he wanted to try, with him doing all the talking, of course, and me occasionally handing him sheets of paper on which he'd written notes and printed out pictures of some of the celebrity A-listers.

"Is Bango coming in with us?" I asked.

"No, of course not, what's the matter with you?"

"It just sounds very... performance-based, what you want to do in these meetings."

"Don't you get it yet? You've always got to put on a show."

"Oh."

"You can't ever stop, Tommy. They don't want the real you. They want the front. They want the player."

Bango squeaked his red nose and his big shoes exploded in a shower of sparks and smoke.

The limo pulled up to a lot and security came out and checked our names. I wasn't even certain which studio we were at. They all looked alike unless you were working there. Groups of tourists made the rounds and crisscrossed in front of the limo. The driver parked in front of an office and Monty and I climbed out. Bango had poured himself another big glass of Jack Daniels. He saluted me with it and I closed the door.

"You know the part you play?" Monty asked me.

"The part of the writer?"

"The part in our presentation. You remember what I told you?"

"Sure," I said.

WHAT MAKES YOU DIE

I had no idea what he'd told me. Things weren't going to work out the way Monty planned. They never did. And I didn't much care, which made life precious and appealing to me for the first time in years.

I realized my hands were empty. I'd left my briefcase behind, thank Christ. I walked side by side with Monty through the corridors of power in Hollywood. We came to another security desk and were told we were cleared. We got stopped again at a secretary's desk and we sat and waited for ten minutes, digesting our red meat. Monty murmured to himself and looked at the top page of the five copies of the screenplay he held. He smiled to himself.

We were told to come in. Monty jumped up so quickly both his knees cracked loud as gunshots. We followed somebody's assistant to a completely glassed-in meeting room. I always preferred the ancient stone and wood of New York to the plastic and glass of Los Angeles. I didn't quite understand why a city given to earthquakes would build with so much glass, but it was just one of the many things about L.A. that was well beyond me.

Waiting for us around an enormous glass table were four power players in suits and Trudy.

Monty didn't remember her. He had the amazing capacity to forget people and circumstances, like being cuffed to a bed with a spider monkey dancing on his forehead.

One of the suits stood and introduced the others. When he got to Trudy, he said, "And our senior rep in charge of creative acquisitions, Trudy Galloway."

Monty had been wrong about no one actually being named Trudy. So had I.

He did all the talking. He started to make his pitch. He had his little skit down cold. His timing was perfect. He nailed a few smart jokes and immediately eased into the hard sell in a sharp way. I liked the way he was presenting himself. He went on for five minutes and still hadn't mentioned a word about *What Makes You Die*.

Trudy looked at me. Her features were angled into a relatively warm expression. It could've meant anything. It could mean she wanted me. It could mean she wanted to destroy me. It could be she was waiting for me to take over from Monty if I ever wanted to get anywhere in the world again.

The suits did what suits do. They did nothing. They showed no significant interest. Their faces were well-hydrogenated and passive. They had perfected the art of making everyone else in Hollywood feel unnecessary and impotent. There was only one good thing about having lost my career, landing in the nuthatch, and living in my ma's basement as polka music subliminally leeched into my brain. I had absolutely nothing to lose.

Bango ran in with a seltzer bottle and started spraying it around. Security was on him in ten seconds, but not before he got his shoes off and started hitting the suits in their heads. The security bulls dragged him out while he clutched his horns and awoogaed like crazy. His eyes met mine and he gave me a wink.

It took a while for everybody to settle down. If nothing else, it had ruined their perfect heads of hair. They frowned and murmured. It had to have been part of Monty's plan all along. He was smart and pretended he didn't know the clown. He straightened his tie and prepared to throw himself back into his pitch.

Trudy glanced at me again. There was still a tinge of sadness in her eyes, but the melancholy gaze was gone. I was glad for her. The raven hair had grown out a little, but the slightly more demure curls still framed her heart-shaped face. Like the first time I'd seen her, she wasn't quite smiling and wasn't quite grinning, and yet was clearly amused by what was going on.

She turned to me and said, "Tom, why don't you tell us about the project?"

Monty practically gagged. He was just about to really get sailing into his big push. He tried to make an excuse for me. He said I was jet-lagged, that I had spent the morning reading to blind kids at the Shriners Hospital for Children, and my voice couldn't possibly hold up.

Trudy said, "Tell us something about the film, Tom."

So I did. I knew exactly what to say about the script and how to make the pitch. After all, I had written the fucker. I knew every word of it. It had brewed and baked at the back of my head for a couple of years. My subconscious had reworked plot twists, denouements, and dialogue five hundred times. I remembered the writing now. I had forgotten it for the same reason that I had forgotten my brother Bobby picking up Kathy and me on a cold rainy day. Because it was something that had happened so often it didn't stand out. I was a writer. There was no other me.

I made my presentation. It was a barn burner. Monty passed the script around to everybody. The suits laughed at my jokes, and they grew thoughtful when I played the contemplative card. I remembered all their names and pointedly spoke to each one of them in turn. I made eye contact. I showed no fear. There was no fear to show. They couldn't hurt me.

Afterward, the suits got up and we all shook hands and everybody filed out, including Monty. He had to go get Bango out of the security lockup or wherever they held mean clowns.

Trudy maneuvered her way in front of me and turned to face me. We looked at each other in the enormous glass room.

I asked, "You wouldn't happen to have the key to four handcuffs, would you?"

"That's got to be the best opening line I've ever heard," she said.

"You've done well for yourself. Becoming head of... whatever the heck your title is."

"I managed to hang in there."

My next comment was obvious. "I didn't."

The melancholy returned, a summer storm in her eyes, and then they cleared. "You're still alive. In this town, that counts for something." She reached over and took my hand gently. I grasped hers a little tighter than I probably should have, but she didn't gasp and she didn't pull away. "Well, whatever you did, it worked. This is a brilliant screenplay. It'll make a hell of a good movie. And a lot of money."

"Maybe."

"Maybe. Hopefully. But I think it will, and I'm good at my job. You'll get a nice, hefty check." She mentioned a number. It was a more than fair number. Once, it would have meant success and validation to me. Now it just meant... I didn't know what it meant, but it didn't mean the same thing anymore, and that was probably a good thing.

"Despite Monty's negotiation skills?"

"Ah, Monty Stobbs, the dear heart... he doesn't even remember me."

"Don't take it personally. The fact that he doesn't remember the woman who cuffed him to a bed in a reindeer outfit with a spider monkey just proves the kind of life Monty lives on a day-to-day basis."

"And you?" she said. "I've heard things. Rumors. How's your life on a day-to-day basis?"

"Today's looking pretty good so far, thanks to you," I said. "I mean that. Thank you."

"You did the work. You wrote a terrific script. You might be able to get a little more at one of the bigger studios."

"I think I'd like to stay here for the time being."

"I think I would like that very much too."

She walked me out. We shook hands outside the glass meeting room and met each other's eyes and left it like that.

I took the elevator down and found Monty and Bango waiting in the lobby. Bango's mouth was bleeding but he was smiling and he awoogaed his happiness. I clapped him on the shoulder. Monty bitched me out about not sticking to his plan. I told him the number Trudy was going to pay us. He said, "Holy fucknuts, that's sweet! Can I work a deal or can I work a deal, baby?" Bango weep-wahhed some more.

Monty wanted to splurge on escorts and champagne. I told him no. I had to find a new apartment. I had to get back to work. There were more movies to write. And maybe novels, and maybe even poetry.

I wondered if Eva might want to leave Hoboken and the witches and the emo-leather-deathers and her roommate behind. It was a lot to ask, considering we'd only known each other a few days. She might say no. That wouldn't kill me either.

The limo maneuvered out of the studio lot. Tiny trains full of tourists went drifting by. I saw old folks who would die before getting back to Peoria and a lot of fresh faces full of rage and passion. Maybe I'd get a place big enough for my ma, my sister, and my grandmother to come live. I looked at Bango and said, "What's your name, man?" He answered, "Will."

I'd managed to get off my knees, even if I'd had to crawl through the madhouse, through several of them, in order to do it. It proved I was still alive, and in this town, in any town, that was something. That was how Hollywood functioned. Where film made the dead eternal, and where love and pain lasted on celluloid forever. It was the land of make-believe, where you had to make yourself real. I was still working on it.

About the Author

Tom Piccirilli is the author of more than twenty novels, including *The Last Kind Words*, which bestselling author Lee Child called "Perfect crime fiction." He's won two International Thriller Awards and four Bram Stoker Awards, as well as having been nominated for the Edgar, the World Fantasy Award, the Macavity, and Le Grand Prix de L'Imaginaire. Learn more about Tom at: www.thecoldspot.blogspot.com.

About the Artist

Danni Kelly is a designer and digital illustrator who will occasionally dabble in poetry. She is often spotted frolicking through the local grocery stores of the Bay Area, admiring packaging design on the shelves. Some of her work can be spotted on *Dark Faith: Invocation*, and Chris Claremont's ebooks *Dragon Moon* and *FirstFlight*. She also sometimes goes by "Spookie", and her work can be found at Behance.net/spookie.

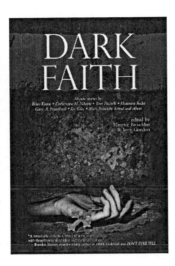

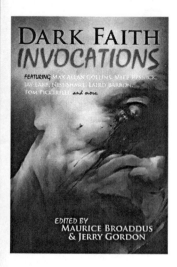